D1308084

"Alas! the grim legion of sepulchral terrors cannot be regarded as altogether fanciful—but, like the Demons in whose company Afrasiab made his voyage down the Oxus, they must sleep, or they will devour us—they must be suffered to slumber, or we perish."

EDGAR ALLAN POE, *THE PREMATURE BURIAL*

INDIAN
SUMMER

AARON MAHNKE

CHAPTER ONE

"What the hell is this place?"

No one else was speaking and the silence was becoming overwhelming.

"Guys?"

The boys stood in the shadow of a doorway, peering into the dark, crypt-like space at the bottom of the stairs. One of them held a gas camping lantern in front of his chest, and he turned it toward the others.

"Say something, guys," he muttered weakly. "What do you think this place was?"

The tallest of the group shuffled on his feet slightly before he turned to face the one holding the lantern.

"I don't know, Mikey," he whispered. His voice warbled slightly. "It doesn't look safe. It looks like an animal's den. It's...I feel like we're not supposed to be here...like we're trespassing or something."

"We *shouldn't* be here, Hank" said a third. His round face was splashed with the hard glow of light from the lantern. He wasn't looking at the others, though, but rather into the dark room, and his eyes were full of fear. "I told you we shouldn't come in this place."

They had known they were trespassing from the moment they stepped onto the property. The fence had long since rotted into a skeletal heap at the rear of the building, and it had been almost too easy to step over it. The moment they had, though, they all felt it, like an unseen watch dog glaring at them from across the litter-strewn lot. Their presence had not been welcome.

It had been Hank Phillips' idea, really. As a general rule, whenever seven teenage boys found themselves bored on a Saturday afternoon in early October, one thing you could count on was that they'd find the worst thing imaginable to alleviate that feeling.

"Let's explore the old Clements place," Hank had suggested.

They had been squatting in the woods behind Bill McCarthy's house near Abbott Park, scratching at the dirt with sticks. Mike had managed to draw a penis and Roger was giggling at it. Bill had smoothed the earth in front of his feet to perfection and was delicately writing his name in evenly spaced capital letters.

"Are you kidding?" Bill spat back. "That place is a death-trap. Everyone knows that, dumb-ass."

Hank tossed his stick at Bill, and it crashed across his name, obscuring some of the letters.

"Hey!" Bill whined. "Cut it out, man!"

"Let's do it," added Mike Barton. "My mom won't be calling me to dinner for another couple of hours anyway. Let's get inside and explore."

"It'll be dark in there," said Roger O'Connor.

"My dad has a lantern in the shed," suggested Bill. "He bought it last year for a camping trip we took with the Scouts. Give me a couple minutes to grab it and fuel it up."

Bill took off in the direction of his house, and vanished around the corner of an old shed that stood near the far end of the yard. Hank stood up and brushed a brown leaf off of his jeans while Mike scuffed his foot across the drawing he had made. Roger frowned disapprovingly.

George Ashcroft and Kenny Tobey, the youngest of the group by almost a year, were pacing anxiously among the trees.

"Why the mill?" asked Kenny. He furrowed his brow, making his already dark eyes seem black. "I've heard it's haunted. My dad said people died in there."

"Yeah," added George. "Some big fire a long time ago, I think."

"No one's used that building for a really long time, guys," said Steve Bowers. "I bet there are animals living inside. We could get hurt." He flashed a wide grin and stood up.

"Don't be a chicken, Steve," said Mike.

Bill stepped back into the circle with the lantern he had promised in one hand and a smirk on his face.

"All filled up," he said cheerfully, holding it up for the others to see. It was a Coleman, crafted of metal and glass, and looked brand new. The base resembled a cherry red tea kettle with a round metal cap for the fuel tank. The bulbous glass was mounted atop a narrow aluminum neck, and on top of it sat a red metal cap. The sharp scent of kerosene met their noses.

"Cool!" Roger exclaimed. He reached out to take it from Bill, but Mike beat him to it.

"Just be careful, Mikey," Bill told him as he grabbed the long metal handle that looped over the top. "My dad will kill me if this gets scratched."

"Don't worry, Bill," Mike said confidently, taking the metal and glass device. "Let's get going, then!"

The old Clements mill building was a little less than a mile to the south of Bill's house, and the group followed the Hollesley River to get there. The river was wide and shallow, and because the tide was out, most of the river's bottom was exposed for the gulls and occasional heron. The smell of rotting fish and salt water was heavy in the air.

When they reached the small bridge that cut across a narrower spot in the river, connecting the older side of Hollesley to the newer developments, they climbed up the bank and then ran across Cordwain Street before dropping back down to the river. Another hundred yards down river they finally caught their first glimpse of the Clements building.

It sat low and squat on the southern bank, across from where the slow trickle of the Port River joined the Hollesley. The windows were tall and narrow, and much of the glass had been broken out over the years, giving the brick facade the appearance of a skull. Vines climbed up the sides of the building in some places, and the foundation had crumbled in others.

The boys headed south along the western side of the property, following the remnants of the fence until they located a section that had deteriorated more severely than the rest. Wood fencing lay on the cement like discarded bones, and they had to avoid rusted nails as they climbed over to the other side where a small lot waited.

Abraham Clements had purchase the property in 1758, just a year after the town had been incorporated, and he had built a small workshop of stone and wood there on the banks of the river. Like many of the workshops in the area, Clements manufactured shoes, depending on the river for access to the port where he was able to ship his goods down to Boston.

He did well for himself, but it had been his son Jeremiah, who took over after his father passed away, that had moved the mill into the industrial age in 1811. He completely replaced the old stone shack with a then-modern brick monolith that had become common of New England manufacturing. The expansion paid off, and at its peak the company employed nearly three hundred men and women.

Then, in 1854, a fire brought an end to the business, as well as the lives of nearly two-dozen employees. Gutted and abandoned, the mill building had stood untouched and forgotten for well over a century. There had been the occasional rumor that someone planned to acquire the property, but nothing ever came of it and the brick husk along the river quickly faded into memory. It now stood as nothing more than a dark shape against the cool New England autumn sky, a shadow of what it once was.

Mike was the first to cross the ruined lot, followed closely by Hank and Roger. George and Kenny followed quickly, with Steve close behind. Bill was the slowest, not because he wasn't fit enough or able to keep up, but because he was so deliberate. Where the others ran blindly across the broken pavement, Bill chose each step carefully, avoiding the shards of glass and metal debris that lay hidden in the weeds. The rest of the group had been peering in through one of the cavernous windows for a moment before Bill finally arrived to join them.

"Don't hurry, Bill," Hank said mockingly, slapping the latecomer on the back.

"How are we getting in?" asked Roger. His pale, round face was flush from the run, though it could just as easily have been because of his Irish heritage.

Without answering, Mike handed the lantern to Bill. Then, he turned back to the window and reached his hands into the darkness. The sill was roughly as high as his chest and at least two feet deep. He had to stand on his toes to get his arms far enough inside. Once he found the inner sill, he pulled himself up and brought his knees onto the cold stone.

"Like this," he grinned. "It's pretty messy in there, but the floor looks strong. I think it's cement." He dropped inside, and they could hear the sound of glass grinding underneath his feet. Slowly, the others followed him through the window, and after waiting for Bill to hand over the lantern and find the perfect grip, all seven boys had left the sunny lot behind.

The interior looked even worse than the outside of the building, if that were possible. Cobwebs and dust covered everything, and though the space was mostly empty, small piles of charred debris littered the floor. Some of the litter looked random, but some of it had the appearance of a nest built by some small animal.

The fire that brought Clements to an end had licked the beams and walls, leaving a deep blackness on everything it touched. The smell of mildew filled their noses, and water was dripping somewhere in a far corner of the room. It was a temple to decay and ruin, and it chilled each of them to the bone.

The burnt remains of some offices leaned against the stone wall in one corner, and a few stairs still clung like rotten teeth to a runner that rose toward a small doorway about fifteen feet up. The vast majority of the large, open factory floor was covered in low, wide tables and the occasional cluster of what looked like shelves.

Directly across the maze of charred tables and debris, on the far wall from where they stood, a large, dark square could be seen, like a gaping mouth.

Mike pointed to the opening. "There," he declared softly. "Let's see what's in that room." He took a step, but then turned when Bill caught his attention.

"The lantern, Mikey," he interrupted. "We'll need the light in there." Bill seemed to shiver when he pointed at the large opening across from them.

"Right," Mike replied, and set the lantern on the floor while Bill pulled a matchbook from his pocket.

When the wick was lit and the matches were stowed safely away, they began the short trip across the factory floor. They had no trouble navigating the space, but nonetheless each of them could feel a subtle oppression that grew stronger with each step.

None of them seemed to like it inside the building, least of all Kenny. He had heard enough frightening tales from his father to have deep anxiety about this new adventure. His bowels churned and goose flesh broke out on his arms. He kept his fears to himself, though, as he always did. The other boys were older, and he didn't want to be seen as weak or afraid.

The room beyond the massive doorway was dark and oppressive. The ceiling was much lower than the main space, and there wasn't a single window. Two long wooden tables ran along one side of the room, though they were badly burned and one leaned heavily toward the wall. Black lumps, presumably boxes, were piled beneath them.

Across from where they all stood, another doorway greeted them. This one was so black that it seemed to devour the light from their lantern. Mike raised it higher as if to ward off the darkness.

"Let's keep going," he said, but his voice has lost much of the confidence that he had shown earlier.

"Look at the size of these tables," wondered Hank. "My dad would kill for a workbench this long." He reached out and lightly touched the table nearest to him, and it instantly toppled into a heap of black wood. Hank turned to glance at the Mike, who offered him a wide-eyed, fearful expression.

"We should get out of here, guys," said Bill. He was checking his clothes for soot and glancing around the room apprehensively. "What if a wall does that?"

Mike ignored him and moved toward the new doorway. He led the way with the lantern held in front of his chest, and the rest of the boys followed him. They had little choice, though; if they didn't want to be left in the dark, they would have to stay close to Mike.

The floor beyond this next doorway seemed to fall away and vanish into blackness, but Mike quickly realized that this new room was actually a stairway leading down to the left. The steps were stone, and though they wore the same layer of black dust that the rest of the building's interior did, it was clear that they had seen better days.

The steps led them to the remains of a large door that blocked off more than half of the opening. It was the kind of door that hung from a track above the doorway, but it no longer moved. It was crafted of thick sheets of iron, covered in rust now, which were held together with large rivets.

Roger pushed against the door to move it out of their way. There was a sickening crack from above them, and the track snapped off the lintel, dropping the heavy door to the floor. He and the others moved away, and someone toward the back of the group let out a small cry of surprise.

The door tottered for a moment before settling upright against the doorframe, slightly more to the right than before. A thick cloud of ash and dust billowed up from the darkness, looking almost like smoke by the light of the lantern, before dissipating to reveal a crowded, chaotic room beyond the gap.

It was this room that frightened them. They all agreed on it, even years later. It was this room that had entranced them and lured them and trapped them. Whether it was the spirits of the dead in that hollow place, or the workings of their subconscious, all seven of the boys felt a pull. One by one, they slipped into the room, following Mike's lantern like a group of cave explorers tethered to each other with a rope.

The seven boys slipped through the narrow gap in the doorway and spread out to explore. It was a small room, no larger than a dozen feet in either direction, and made to feel even smaller by the seemingly countless piles of burnt debris that huddled in large clumps in various parts of the room. No other doorways or windows could be seen; the room was a dead end.

"Look at this," Kenny said, picking up a metal object about the size of a screwdriver. "I think this is an awl." The metal was green with corrosion, but the point still looked as sharp as ever.

"Makes sense," muttered Steve, who seemed to be afraid to speak to loudly. "They made shoes here, right? At least, that's what I've heard. Aren't those things used to poke holes in leather?"

Kenny nodded and set the tool down. "I don't see any leather, though."

"Duh," said Steve. "There was a fire in here, dumb-ass. Leather burns."

"Don't be a dick, Steve," George added. He was always defending Kenny. The two were a year behind the others in school and had known each other long before they joined up with the other boys. "It's creepy in here. I can barely think straight, myself."

"You never think straight, Georgie," said Hank from across the room. "That's why we like you." Hank grinned, but George could only see the dim flash of his teeth in the darkness.

Kenny picked the awl back up and dug the point into one of the piles beneath the table. What he saw made him dig harder. "Hey guys," he said excitedly. "I think there's unburnt leather under the crust on top."

Mike brought the lantern over to help illuminate Kenny's work. Roger and Bill joined them, though Hank and the others were close by. Kenny caught the end of a piece of leather and teased it out from the bundle. It was pale and stiff, but seemed to be untouched by the flames.

He was about to reach out to grab the material with his bare hand when Roger bent close and caught him by the wrist. "Don't," he said curtly. "Look." He pointed to the pile that Kenny had been slowly breaking apart with the awl, and at the sharp white objects protruding from it.

Kenny immediately fell backwards, kicking his feet to backpedal from the debris. "Bones!" he cried out in panic. "Those are bones!"

In much the same way that Mike's confidence had been contagious in the moments leading up to their entrance to the old mill building, Kenny's fit of terror and panic sent the group of young teens into a frenzy. Mike fumbled the lantern and nearly dropped it before regaining control, and then lunged toward the doorway.

"Run!" someone shouted, and each boy snapped out of his paralyzed trance and bolted toward the exit. Mike was the first to slip through, taking the light with him. Bill followed close behind, and then Hank. By the time Steve and Roger made it through the gap in the door, Mike was already at the top of the stairs, and darkness was quickly engulfing the lower room.

The last to run for the door were George and Kenny. While the others ran out of fear and panic, George had stayed to help his friend off the floor. In that brief instant, the room had become dark enough that both boys struggled to find the direction they needed to run. They seemed trapped, and panic welled up in Kenny's chest.

George glanced around and saw a glimmer of light. He caught Kenny's arm and bolted for the door, dragging his friend behind him. He barely managed to squeeze through the opening, but because the room was so dark, Kenny ran straight into the iron door.

There was a wet thud as the boy's head bounced off the heavy metal plating and his arm slipped free from George's grip. His friend turned to help him as he crumpled into an unconscious heap on the dirty floor. The sound of breaking stone above his head stopped him in his tracks, though.

Chaos seemed to erupt. The heavy door, knocked off balance by Kenny's impact, began a slow-motion fall backward into the room. At the same moment, the stone lintel of the doorframe gave way and decades-old brick and mortar rained down upon the bottom of steps.

George scrambled backwards and managed to escape higher up the steps and avoid the debris, but Kenny was not as fortunate. The door landed on his limp body, crushing him beneath its weight, and then the rubble from the collapsing doorframe fell on top of it. There was no cry of pain, just the rumble of bricks crashing onto iron.

"Kenny!" George cried out. He wanted to rush back and find his friend, but the ceiling of the stairway was rupturing upward. Fear took hold and his feet pushed him up the steps, one by one, as bricks fell behind him, chasing him out of the darkness.

He fell on the floor of the next room and sobbed uncontrollably as the dust of the collapse settled on his back. "Kenny!" he cried out again. "No...no...no!"

The others quickly surrounded him and managed to pull him to his feet.

"Where's Kenny!" Mike implored, glancing back at the dark stairway. "What happened?"

"The door," George sobbed. His chest heaved and tears cut glossy tracks down his dirty face. "The door...it fell on him...the wall caved in..."

"Oh no," whispered Hank. "Oh God, no."

"We've got to get out of here, George," Mike said, tugging on the boy's arms. "The rest of the building could come down on us, man. We'll go get help. We'll find Kenny and get him out, you'll see. Come on, George."

Mike put an arm around George's shoulders, and Steve helped guide him out the door and across the main factory floor. No one spoke. They moved in silence as quickly as they could toward the window they had climbed in through. The only sound they could hear was the occasional rumble as more of the stairway collapsed in the room behind them.

Once outside, they hurried back along the river, back to Bill's house, to get help. Nothing could help Kenny, though. Kenny was lost.

CHAPTER TWO

Mike woke with a start. It was still dark outside and the room was much colder than it had been when he had climbed into bed. *How long had it been?* he thought. He reached over for his phone to check the time. *Lovely. Only 3:00 a.m.*

There was no point in trying to go back to sleep. Mike hadn't slept well for a long time. Not since that day in the mill. How could he, when every dream took him back and forced him to relive that experience over and over again?

Mike sat up and felt for his t-shirt on the floor near the bed. Tugging it over his head, he stumbled toward the bathroom and flicked on the yellow fluorescent light above the mirror. For a moment he just stood there, trying to recognize the stranger looking back at him in the reflection, and then he moved to the toilet where he emptied his bladder.

"If she were still alive, I doubt my own mother would recognize me," he said out loud to no one at all. He glanced into the mirror again. His short dark hair was sprinkled with gray, and wrinkles had surrounded his eyes. He looked like a man ten years older than the thirty-five summers he had seen. He wasn't surprised, though. He knew what had aged him so drastically.

That day twenty years ago at the Clements Mill had done something to him. Perhaps it was the brutal catastrophe of losing a friend, or the trauma he endured leading that group of broken, frightened boys out of the mill and back to Bill McCarthy's house. Those were both good possibilities, but Mike had other ideas. He blamed that room.

The room had seemed to lure them in. That darkness had taunted them and stolen their courage. In the end, the room had taken the life of Kenny Tobey, and in doing so, it had robbed the other six boys of whatever youth they possessed.

It had taken them ten minutes to run back to Bill's house that late afternoon in October of 1993, but it had felt like an eternity. Bill had burst into the kitchen and breathlessly informed his mother of what happened, his words slurred by sobs and panic. The afternoon quickly erupted with activity.

Shortly after, rescue personnel attempted to enter the lower room of the building and retrieve Kenny's body, holding on to the slim hope that he might still be alive, but the amount of debris prevented the first responders from making it any farther than the room above.

It took a local construction crew another 9 hours to shore up the stairs and excavate their way down before a team of Hollesley EMTs could enter the room. Kenny's body was found crushed beneath what was estimated to be a half-ton of brick and timber, all of which rested on the iron door. It was clear that he had died instantly, long before his friends had exited the mill and run for help.

Mike's parents were furious, of course. They berated his judgment and heaped blame on him and his friends for what they called a "god-awful, horrible stunt". But they also saw the pain in their son's eyes and tempered their discipline with comfort. The death of Kenny seemed punishment enough, something that was true for all of the boys.

The funeral, held just one week after the accident, was the most difficult part of that dark autumn. It was the first time that all six of the boys had gathered together since their parents picked them up at Bill's house that dark afternoon. Their reunion was bitter, and while they spent their time near each other, very little conversation took place. Something dark had climbed in between them, isolating each one of them.

Nothing could capture the loss that Kenny's father had experienced, though. His wife had passed away just two years prior, a victim of a hit and run accident near Beverly Hospital where she worked as a nurse. Now, Daniel Tobey had lost his only son. Much like that iron door, the crushing weight of his loss could be felt throughout that long afternoon in the funeral home.

Due to the nature of Kenny's death, the casket was closed to viewing, even for family. With no body to view and grieve over, each of the six boys made it a point to visit with Mr. Tobey and share their heartfelt condolences while barely managing to keep their feelings of guilt and failed responsibility hidden beneath the surface. Mr. Tobey was cold and vacant, though, failing to even thank them for coming.

It had been the funeral that had given birth to the intense sorrow, guilt, and shame that Mike now felt rooted deep in his soul. And now, twenty years later, he and the others would be reuniting for another funeral. Another of their own had died, and suddenly the chasm of time and pain that had kept them apart for so long had been bridged.

They hadn't made any particular effort to drift apart, of course, but spending time together had quickly become much less enjoyable than before. It had become impossible to be together and not feel Kenny's absence. They wanted life to carry on, of course, and they knew that they still needed each other in some broken way. Each time they came together, however, it only served to magnify the pain and guilt that each of them felt.

So each went their separate way, and soon high school and then college had made the diaspora complete. That was all about to change, though. Everything was about to change.

On a typical day, Mike would head into the office early. He was always the first to arrive at work. Everyone thought it was because he was punctual and driven and wanted to set a good example for the rest of the office. Mike was happy to let them believe that, of course.

It was much better than explaining that he arrived early each day because he woke each night panting and sweating from the nightmare rooted in his childhood; a nightmare that repeated itself over and over again. No, Mike went to the office early each day because it was his way of escaping all of that.

This had given Mike an edge over his peers early on, and after joining the accounting firm a decade prior, he had quickly risen through the ranks to become one of the company's top managers. Some even whispered that he was in line for yet another promotion, but there were always whispers like that, and Mike tried to ignore them. He just wanted to work. The harder he worked, the less he thought of the nightmares.

Today, though, Mike's mind was on other things. George Ashcroft, one of his friends from that day at the mill twenty years ago, had died. It didn't seem possible—George was barely halfway through his thirties and had so much life left ahead of himself—yet it was true.

What made it even harder to comprehend was that he had seen George just a few days earlier. He had been making one of his frequent runs to pick up coffee from the Midtown Café for his team at the office. It had been a warm day, the kind of day that people still call an Indian Summer, and very out of character with the rest of the cool autumn that they had been experiencing.

Mike had slipped out of the seat of his car and was closing the door behind him when a face caught his eye. There was that moment where the face didn't register. Not on the conscience level, at least. Sure, something about the face stood out to him, connected with him and begged for notice, but Mike wasn't aware of why that might be. Still, he stopped for a second and looked harder at the man.

He was shorter than Mike by a few inches and had shaggy brown hair. He was fit and slender, and everything about him seemed youthful but his face, which was lined and weathered. The man had been exiting the café with a coffee in one hand and a phone in the other, and had stopped to look down at the little screen for a moment.

Something inside Mike's mind had clicked, and then recognition flooded over him.

"George!" he exclaimed, a smile working its way onto his face. "George Ashcroft?" he added in a questioning tone, just to be safe.

The man looked up, and for a moment he seemed confused and maybe even indifferent, but then the same recognition crept over his features as well.

"If it isn't Mike Barton," he said with a smile that seemed pained, but still genuine. "Wow, it's been quite a while, hasn't it?"

"Absolutely," Mike replied. "What, eight years?"

"Yeah, I think so," George replied, working through the math at the same time. "Our ten-year high school reunion, right?"

"Oh man," Mike smiled. "Don't remind me. Our twentieth is creeping up a bit too fast, and nothing makes me feel older than adding twenty years to my memories of high school."

The two men laughed in the way that two men do when they're looking to lighten the mood, but there was a pregnant pause where nothing was said. A motorcycle with an exhaust system that was far too forgiving rumbled by. A family walked around them to enter the café. It was George who broke the silence.

"So, uh..." He faltered, as if the rest was too difficult. "I just bumped into Kenny's dad in there," he almost whispered. "Seems like today is a day for reunions, maybe?"

"Wow, really?" Mike said with disbelief. "I don't think I've seen him in years." He thought about it for a few seconds before adding, "Maybe since the accident."

Mike always referred to what happened at the mill as 'the accident', but he knew it was a lie he told himself to deal with his role in those events. *There was nothing accidental about it*, he told himself. *You talked them into it. You led them there. Accidents are random. This...this was your fault.*

George nodded, and then forced another smile, though it was more apparent this time. "I haven't either. He seems well, though. I don't think he's changed a bit."

The two men continued to make small talk for a few minutes. They chatted about their jobs, their families, and the rest of their old gang, but it was clear to both men that their past still had power over them. They soon parted ways, promising (as old friends newly reunited often do) to get in touch again soon and maybe to grab a drink. Mike knew that was unlikely to happen, though.

Mike waited outside the café while George walked to his car, got in, and drove off. Then, with one last glance at the door of the restaurant, he turned and walked back to his car. His team could skip their afternoon coffee for once; there was no way in hell he was going to knowingly walk into a conversation with Kenny's father. Not now, after all these years. The wound was still too raw and the guilt too heavy.

Looking back now he wished he had made different choices. Maybe he should have grabbed a coffee for himself and sat George down and talked longer. Mike wasn't sure how helpful that would have been for George, but he was sure it would have done wonders for his own conscience. To have someone else to share his burden with would have been very comforting.

Now, though...well, that opportunity was gone. He wondered how many of the others would be at the funeral today. Bill would be; he was the one who called Mike and told him about George, after all. Mike couldn't help but wonder if he would see all of them at the funeral home. It had been a very long time since they had all been in the same room together. Maybe it had been long enough, though.

It was like removing a bandage, in a way. When you get a cut, you bandage it and protect it, even though it still hurts like hell. After a while, though, most cuts will heal enough to make the bandage unnecessary. And that's when you have to rip it off. It hurts, but in the end it might be better than keeping the wound covered up.

Maybe today would be the day that they all finally took their bandages off.

* * *

Weekends had a way of making Hollesley feel like a sleepy little town. Not that it was a small town; the population had topped out at around sixteen thousand a few years ago, and it was still a thriving place like many of the cities in the area north of Boston known as Cape Ann.

A Walgreens had recently been built across the street from the new CVS in the middle of town and there were very few empty storefronts on Main Street compared to other towns in the area. But even healthy towns wake up a bit sleepy on Saturday morning.

Early October usually has a way of lulling people to sleep. Daylight Savings Time was still a few weeks away from ruining the lives of parents across the country, and the leaves had only just started to change. It rained often and the sky seemed to oscillate between brilliantly clear and heavily overcast.

As a result, most October mornings seemed dark and tired. Once the trees managed to trade their fading greens for the brilliant oranges, reds, and yellows that New England was so revered for, things would start to feel a bit more festive and alive. Right now, though, it could be a bit depressing.

If Mike were a normal person, he would have slept in on a day like this, but Mike hadn't slept late on a Saturday since he was fifteen. Instead, he had climbed out of bed around 3:00 a.m. and made himself a light breakfast before beginning a bit of house cleaning. He lived alone, and even though he didn't pay someone to clean his home — something he could well-afford to do, considering his income — he preferred to handle the responsibility himself.

Mike liked to care for things. He had a small greenhouse in the back yard where he got to nurture and grow a few of his favorite vegetables. With the winter months fast approaching he was growing spinach, broccoli, snap peas, and Swiss chard. The structure was nothing more than a transparent shed constructed of plywood and clear polyvinyl sheets, but it gave him something to do and he usually enjoyed the results.

He could be found in the greenhouse most days once the sun was up, watering and pruning as needed. From inside he had a clear view of the eastern sky, and today the horizon seemed to glow with a deep pink hue.

Red skies in the morning, sailors take warning, he thought. *I wonder what storm this day has in store for me.*

Mike didn't like to be pessimistic, but he held himself to a pretty high standard in most areas of life. When he failed to meet those expectations, he blamed himself. And Mike was a pro at blaming himself.

If he were to win an award for making everything his own fault, he'd do pretty damn well. He wasn't really a failure—not by the standards of others, at least. He had a good paying job, a nice car, and a well-kept house. He was a middle-class success.

Mike had skewed standards, though, and he knew why. He felt a heightened sense of responsibility for what happened that day in the mill, and it had defined his life. It was the ghost of Kenny, haunting him decades later.

Sure, the counselors had been telling him otherwise for years. They were insistent that each of the six surviving boys should be experiencing what they referred to as the 'bystander effect'. That was a fancy way of saying that the more people around to observe a tragic event, the less responsibility each one feels to help.

Mike didn't know how the others felt, but he knew that the idea sounded like complete bunk to himself. What happened at the Clements place was his fault. He was certain of that. The guilt had followed him around like a shadow for two decades.

Being this hard on himself carried over into the normal parts of his life. Mike knew that it might not be the healthiest thing, but he had found ways to justify it. He expected the worst, all the time, and usually expected it to be his fault. So if the funeral today were to break down into chaos and pain, it would most likely be due to something Mike did or said.

A vibration in his pocket caught his attention and after wiping his hands on a rag he pulled out his phone. Next to the incoming number was a photo of a balding, middle-aged man. It was Bill McCarthy.

He and Bill had remained the closest over the years, making a point to see each other every few months, sometimes more. Bill seemed very well adjusted, especially considering the emotional mess that Mike perceived himself to be suffering, and that made Bill a calming presence to be around. It didn't hurt that Bill was famous, either.

Well, famous might be too strong of a word. Bill was a writer of thriller and suspense novels. Over the years he had built a strong following across the country. He earned a decent enough living, and he even claimed to receive a steady flow of fan mail of both the digital and paper variety. And the fact that he had moved to Salem, a town renowned for its dark and chilly history, only seemed to lend credence to the professional aura of William J. McCarthy.

They got together for drinks from time to time, usually at a rustic Irish pub near Salem Commons, and had managed to move their conversations far from the events at the Clements factory and into the present. This was a relief to Mike, who welcomed a chance to talk with an old friend about something other than the past, but he also wondered if they had done that intentionally. They might simply have been avoiding the thing that they needed to talk about the most.

Mike tapped the button on his phone's display and brought it to his ear.

"Hey Bill," he answered with a smile. "Isn't it a bit early for a night-owl writer like yourself to be up and about?"

"You're a funny man," Bill responded, and Mike could hear the grin on his face. "For a man that sleeps about four hours each night, you're sure in a good mood. In the greenhouse?"

"You know it. I'll have a basket of broccoli and kale for you next week, by the way. I can't eat all of this myself." Mike walked mindlessly over to a section of the room and ran his hand over the green, ruffled edges of the kale.

"Looking forward to it," Bill replied. "Us single guys tend to eat poorly, but you're helping me buck the system, man. I appreciate your efforts to destroy the stereotype."

"My pleasure," Mike grinned, before returning to the root of the call. "What's up, Bill? Everything all right?"

"Oh, for sure. I just wanted to make sure you were still planning to come today. You know...to George's funeral."

"Of course," Mike replied, trying not to sound hurt while at the same time just processing the fact that Bill might have accepted it if he had decided not to attend.

"Good," Bill said with relief. "The others will be there, you know. All of them."

Mike closed his eyes and took in a deep breath. He felt a strange mixture of relief and panic. He missed these old friends so much, yet had believed for years that they all blamed him for what happened. The notion of seeing them again, together in one place, both excited him and filled him with fear.

"I had wondered...," he started to say, searching for the right words. "I wondered if they would come. No one lives too far away, so it almost seemed like a sure thing."

"Yeah, there was some concern that Hank wouldn't make it," Bill explained, "but that was just an issue with his work schedule and he sorted it out."

"Good to hear," Mike said. "It's been too long."

"Indeed," Bill agreed quickly. "Far too long."

"What time do you plan to get there?" Mike asked.

"A little before noon, I think. It depends on traffic. You know how Salem can be in October."

"Hell yeah," Mike chuckled. "You'd better get headed this way now, in fact. You never know how bad it might be."

He was only half serious. Salem had a reputation as a very supernatural-friendly town, something of an over-correction from the well-known witch trials of the 1692. For a long time that tragedy was repressed and unspoken, until the more enlightened twentieth century, that is.

Sometime in the Seventies the city started to foster a new image, one that portrayed itself as something out of *Bewitched* or *The Munsters*. Those efforts paid off, economically at least, because tens of thousands of tourists now flock to the 'witch city' each October. The numbers grow as the month ticks by until finally everything climaxes on Halloween.

As a result, traffic in Salem is horrendous for most of the month. Between the increase in foot traffic from pedestrian tourists and those brave enough to bring their vehicles, the streets of Salem can seem as congested as the arteries of a competitive hotdog eater. A route that normally would have taken twenty minutes to drive might now take twice that.

"I'll do my best," Bill said with a laugh. "See you later, then."

"Later," Mike replied, and then hung up.

CHAPTER THREE

Mike arrived at the funeral home ten minutes before noon, parking toward the back of the small lot. He took the keys out of the ignition and then stayed in his seat a moment longer, soaking in the silence. He wasn't sure he was ready for the macabre reunion that was about to take place, but he had a feeling deep inside that told him it was for his own good.

Tremblay Funeral Home was a large box of whitewashed brick. A wide portico ran the length of the front, each of the four double columns helping to bear the weight of the flat roof above. Though the majority of the building had originally been a large residence, it had served as one of the main funeral homes in Hollesley for the past century.

A small one-story room had been added to the right side of the building, off of which a carport had been built. The carport now contained the black hearse and a few vehicles that had already lined up behind it for the procession out to the cemetery. Beyond this small addition was the parking lot, bending around the side of the facility to the rear, where more pavement awaited for those funerals that required the space.

Mike had been here a handful of times before. In the fourth grade his maternal grandmother had passed away suddenly and the family had chosen Tremblay as the place for her funeral services. He returned during middle school for the funeral of an older cousin's husband's aunt — or something like that, he was never quite sure — but much of that afternoon was spent out back with a few of the other teenagers, trading turns on a borrowed skateboard and drinking soda from the buffet inside.

The last time he had been here was twenty years ago, for the funeral of Kenny Tobey. Mike was positive that today's funeral would be much more bearable thanks to the numbness that two decades of psychological processing can create. Yet he still knew that today was the emotional successor to that horrific autumn, and he could feel the fear and stress coiled up in his intestines like a burning serpent.

A black Audi sedan pulled up beside his driver-side door, snapping him out of his dark thoughts. It was Bill, and though the man who got out of the car now had much less hair and many more wrinkles, the easy smile and meticulous movements were still very much stereotypical of the Bill McCarthy of old.

Mike lowered his window. "Glad you could make it. New car?"

Bill pressed his thumb against the door handle and a small chirp issued from the car.

"You bet," he smiled. "The old one was getting a bit too dirty, you know?"

Mike chuckled. "You probably throw your socks away after one wear too, don't you?"

"I wear them twice, thank you very much," he smiled.

Mike raised his window and climbed out of the car to join Bill. He was glad for the casual banter.

"How's the new book coming along, Mr. Famous Author?" he asked mockingly as he shook Bill's hand.

"Slow," Bill replied, clearly frustrated. "This one's been a bit harder to tease out of my brain. I'm not ready to declare a full-blown case of writer's block just yet, but I'm certainly fighting for this one."

The two men walked slowly toward the front of the building. The sun was out, though most of the western sky was cloudy and gray, and the sunlight felt good. It felt like it might even reach the low eighties, if the wind played along. *What an odd autumn,* Mike thought.

"Any deadlines or contracts hanging over your head on this one?" he asked, trying to find a solution for his friend.

"Nothing out of the ordinary," he replied, and then corrected himself. "Nothing out of the ordinary for me, I mean. Large advance, tight schedule, etcetera. I normally work fine under pressure like this, so I don't think that's it."

"Well, I hope it gets sorted out. Can't be fun, all that frustration," Mike offered in a conciliatory tone. Just then, another car pulled into the lot and headed in their direction. "That looks like Hank, doesn't it?"

Bill nodded. "Indeed."

The man who got out of the dark Ford sedan was dressed in a deep blue suit that looked tired and well-traveled. His red hair was cut short, and his skin was pale and weathered. Most would say that Hank was 'thick' from the waist up, but he didn't like that. He was muscular, but still carried a bit of baggage from his first years behind the wheel of a police cruiser and the various desks in the department. He could still keep up in the department's weight room, and that was all that mattered as far as he was concerned.

"Hank Phillips," Mike announced with a smile. "How the hell are you, man?" He extended his hand, and Hank grinned before crushing it in a grip that might have injured a black bear.

"I'm good, Mikey," he replied amiably. "How about you? Things good?"

"As good as they can be, I guess," he offered. "Any sign of Steve yet?"

The others shook their heads.

"I talked to him on the phone yesterday and he said he was coming," Bill added. "Maybe he's just stuck in traffic. And Roger is supposed to make it, too. He's never been one to be punctual, though."

Hank chuckled at this. "You're not far from the truth. Roger will most likely show up late to his own funeral."

"And intoxicated beyond all comprehension, right?" Bill added with a forced smile.

Roger had always loved alcohol. He was the one who introduced the rest of the old gang to beer back in middle school. Most of them rarely drank with him, but he seemed to consider a can of Miller High Life to be essential camping gear because he had consistently produced one from his backpack nearly every time they had gathered in the woods behind Bill's house. He would typically pass the can around, allowing anyone to take a drink if they wanted, and then he would finish off the rest himself.

Bill had never seen Roger buy the beer, so he assumed it had been taken from Mr. O'Conner's personal stash in the small refrigerator out in their garage. It wasn't until early high school that Roger moved up to buying it himself, using a fake driver's license he had purchased from Billy Hasworth, one of the older kids who haunted the automotive repair wing of the school. A year or so after the accident Bill had seen a lot less of Roger, but he bumped into him enough back then to know that he was drinking more than beer, and more regularly than just on the weekends.

They hadn't stayed in the tightest of fellowship since they graduated, but he still saw Roger from time to time. He lived in Salem, but many miles and income brackets separated his apartment from Bill's Federal style brownstone in the Chestnut District. Most summer evenings Roger could be found down on Essex Street, near Lappin Park, playing his saxophone with an upturned hat at his feet. Bill always viewed Roger as a work in progress, but whether that progress was construction or demolition was something he just didn't know.

"Let's head in," Hank said decisively. "I'm sure George's family is already inside and they could probably use some distracting conversation, at the very least. Roger and Steve can find their way in when they get here."

The others nodded and followed after him.

Inside the funeral home they were greeted by a pair of middle-aged men dressed in dark suits who introduced themselves as cousins of George, and then were guided into the lobby off the wide hallway. There was a guest book on a small table to one side, and a wide doorway across from it, leading into the overflow area at the back of the chapel.

Bill stopped to sign his name while the others proceeded into the chapel, quietly greeting the few people they recognized as they headed toward the front of the room. When he caught up, Mike was talking to a short woman with greying hair and Hank had moved past them toward the front, where George's body lay inside a closed casket.

It was Margaret Ashcroft, George's mother.

"I am so very, very sorry, Mrs. Ashcroft," Mike was saying. "I saw George just a few days ago. So full of life and humor. I'm," he cut off as Bill approached. "We all are...we...just don't have the words."

Bill nodded in agreement.

"Thank you," she said warmly. "Thank you both. I know George would be so pleased that you came." She smiled, but it seemed well-practiced and cosmetic. There was so much pain and loss below the surface.

"We wouldn't have even considered not coming," came a new voice. Mike turned to see Steve extending his hand to Mrs. Ashcroft, with Roger standing beside him. "George meant a lot to all of us."

"Thank you," she murmured, and then turned as another guest caught her attention and gave her a warm hug.

"Glad you could make it, boys," Hank said as he approached from the front. "Car trouble?"

"Of course," Roger answered. His words were almost imperceptibly slurred, but Mike noticed it. He was pretty sure the others did as well. "Steve was nice enough to come pick me up. My car's in the shop this week and you know how traffic can be in Salem."

"You bet," Bill added in agreement.

Hank looked around at the growing crowd. "Have you guys seen anyone else we might know? And where's George's dad?"

"Over there," Steve said, pointing toward the front of the room where a short man with a receding hairline and dark-framed glasses stood, his back to the casket, while a number of bereaved visitors consoled him.

Without a word the five men walked toward Mr. Ashcroft, who looked up from his conversation and noticed their approach. A smile briefly appeared, but quickly melted back into the face of a mourning father. He excused himself and stepped toward them.

"Well, I'll be," he began softly. "I wasn't sure if you'd come. Thank you. Thank you so much." He reached out and took the first hand he could find—Hank's

—and shook it vigorously. "It's so good to see you all here."

"Not a problem, Mr. Ashcroft," Steve replied with a compassionate smile. "We're glad to be here. Though I know we all wish it were under better circumstances."

"Don't we all," the older man replied. "It's not been easy, believe me. So many unanswered questions. It all feels so fresh. I know we'll make it through this, but it can feel so overwhelmingly dark and hopeless sometimes."

"I can't imagine the pain of losing a child," Bill responded. "We feel the loss of a childhood friend, but I doubt anything can compare to what you are going through. If there's anything you need, Mr. Ashcroft, don't hesitate to ask."

"Please," the man said, "call me Stephen."

"You mentioned that there were questions," Hank cut in. His usually mischievous smile had been replaced with something more professional and serious. "What did you mean by that?"

Stephen sighed heavily. "Honestly? We're not sure how George died," he replied, looking off to the side at the empty space beside Hank and his friends. "All we know is that he was found just north of the Babson Reservoir, near one of those large boulders by the train tracks."

"Why there?" Hank asked, trying to put the pieces together. "Was that unexpected?"

"Oh, no, George loved to hike, and he did a lot of it by himself. That area was one of his favorite places to spend time outdoors."

"Was it a hiking accident, then?" Bill asked, looking for a reason for the mysterious circumstances.

Stephen Ashcroft was visibly pained, and his eyes were wet, but he continued to explain. "A young couple was out hiking early Thursday morning. They're the ones who found George's body. His head had been..." he shuddered as if a cold wind had passed by the back of his neck and closed his eyes for a moment. "His skull had been broken on one of the large boulders."

"Oh God," murmured Mike. "That's horrible."

"One of the Babson Boulders, you mean?" Bill inquired. Stephen nodded numbly. "Which boulder was it?"

The Babson Boulders were an early Twentieth Century addition to a historical site known as the Common Settlement, near Gloucester. The site itself was the center of much legend, mostly centered on witchcraft that sprouted up after the town was abandoned in the early Nineteenth Century. It was called Dogtown, some say, because after all of the people had fled, only their dogs remained.

It was during the Great Depression that a wealthy businessman named Roger Babson paid a number of unemployed stonecutters from Gloucester and the surrounding area to carve short inspirational messages into two-dozen boulders in the Dogtown area. Messages like 'Keep Out of Debt' and 'Get a Job' now greet hikers who visit to enjoy the wooded landscape.

"The one that said 'Save'," he paused, gathering his courage and strength. "But someone had added to it. They wrote with George's blood."

"Christ," whispered Hank, who quickly clapped a hand over his mouth and glanced around. "That's horrible. Did the police tell you what it said?"

Stephen nodded, "*SAVE YOURSELF.*"

"Save yourself?" Hank repeated softly. "Good God, that's insane. The Gloucester police are investigating it further, right?" The professional side of Hank was quickly taking over. "I haven't heard a word about this in my department."

"I'm sure," Stephen replied, "and you probably won't, either. Gloucester is keeping it very quiet. I have a feeling they're afraid of panic. If there's one thing that town could use less of, it's bad publicity. And I can't blame them, but I also want to know what happened."

"So," Mike interrupted, "Are you suggesting that George was killed?"

Stephen shook his head. "We just don't know," he replied. "One idea is that George wrote it himself as he bled to death and confusion overtook him, but I don't think many people could believe that. The detective that I spoke with seemed pretty convinced it was foul-play."

"Who would do such a thing?" Steve asked aloud to no one but himself. "I don't understand. George was so kind, so honest. What could he possibly have done to get himself killed?"

Henry's shoulders slumped as if crushed beneath an immeasurable weight. "I have no idea," he said with a sigh. There was more wetness around his eyes. "I just have no idea."

"Hello, boys," a new voice interrupted from behind them. Bill turned to see a familiar face, but the name was just out of reach. Thankfully Mike was sharper.

"Mr. Tobey," he said with quiet surprise. "I...it's good to see you here."

The man smiled warmly. He was of average height, and though his dark hair was peppered with gray hairs, his face was youthful and strong. He had sharp features that reminded Mike of his son Kenny.

"Hello, Mike," he said. "I doubt you expected to see me, I know." He motioned to Stephen with one hand. "I probably know more than anyone here what this man is going through. I felt it my duty to visit."

"Thank you so much, Daniel," Stephen replied. "That means a lot to me." He glanced around for a moment, and then held up a finger. "Hold on. Let me find Margaret. She'll want to see you as well." Then he disappeared.

"How are you, Mike?" Mr. Tobey asked.

The older man extended a hand, and Mike took it after a moment of hesitation. The last time Mike had spoken to Kenny's father was in this very room during the funeral for his son. He had not been prepared for this. All of a sudden, his heart was racing and he wanted nothing more than to run and hide like a little boy.

"I'm good, sir," he managed to reply. "H-how are you?"

Mr. Tobey didn't answer the question. "Hard to believe it's been twenty years. Seeing you and the others makes me wonder what Kenny would be like now if he were alive today. How tall he would have grown. What kind of work he would be doing. If he would be married or have kids."

"Kenny always told me he wanted to be a scientist," Steve said from Mike's left. "He was a patient kid. I bet he would have been a teacher." He smiled, but there was a distant look in his eyes.

"A teacher," Mr. Tobey echoed out loud. "Yes, I could see that. That's a good assumption, Steve. How's parenthood treating you? Where are you living now?" He grasped Steve's hand and slapped him on the shoulder.

"We're over in the Davidson Street area, across from the middle school," Steve replied. "Parenthood has its ups and downs, but I wouldn't change a thing. Beth does an amazing job with the kids all day, and I work my ass off to keep them fed and clothed. What else can you do, right?"

Mr. Tobey smiled. "That's wonderful. Enjoy the journey. It's over before you know it. Too early, sometimes."

Mike could feel the tension in the air. It was hard to believe that Kenny's father harbored no ill feelings about what happened to his son. He half-expected shouting to break out in the middle of the chapel as two decades of grief burst its seal and exploded over he and his friends.

"Sure thing, Mr. Tobey," Steve replied, and then looked around him at the others. Bill stepped forward and extended a hand.

"Good to see you, Daniel," he said with a quiet voice. "It's been a long time, though that seems to be the theme for today: old acquaintances reunited."

"Has the makings of a great novel, maybe?" the older man suggested. His face was indecipherable.

"There's enough tragedy in this room to fill a few books, I'm sure."

Bill wasn't sure how to respond. The pain and loss in this room was far too personal to tap for inspiration, but he understood what Mr. Tobey meant. At least, he thought he did. *Is this man mocking me?*, he thought.

"That's not my style," he responded flatly. "I think an author would frighten away everyone in their life if they drew inspiration that close to home."

"Don't crap where you live, is that the motto?" the man grinned, but he looked far from amused. "Good advice to live by, I'd wager." Bill could only nod, unsure of what to say in response. "Your books are doing well, I heard. Did fame and fortune take you far from here or did you stay local?"

"Salem," Bill replied. "I managed to find a home on Chestnut Street, which was a small miracle. Near Hamilton Hall."

"Very nice," Daniel replied. "Good to hear you're doing well. Don't forget your roots."

"Never," Bill responded.

The older man then turned and shook hands with Roger. "Still enjoying adult beverages, I see," he said with a hint of disapproval.

Roger grinned, his social acumen dulled slightly by the pre-funeral refreshments he had been enjoying at home. "Everything in moderation, right?"

"I'm sure," Daniel replied.

"I live above a roast beef shop and down the street from a package store," Roger added. "I'm destined to be fat and drunk for the rest of my life." He grinned wide.

"Always the over-achiever," Daniel said before turning to the last of the friends.

Hank seemed to be the only one of the group who didn't whither slightly at the sight of Mr. Tobey. "Glad to have a chance to see you, Hank. How's your dad doing?"

Hank's father had been battling colon cancer for the past three months, keeping the family very busy. Drives to Mass General for chemo, follow-up visits to the oncologist at the local Lahey facility and managing some of the in-home nursing care that he required through it all had become a second job to Hank.

His mother was managing the bulk of the small details like medication and dietary changes, and she looked as if she had aged five years in the short time they had been fighting the cancer. Hank, though, took the majority of the weight on his broad shoulders, and he was fine with that. He liked to do things on his own. He knew it would be done correctly, by the book, and on time. He rarely leaned on others if he could help it.

"He's still in the woods, as they say," Hank said. "We're not going to know if there's been improvement for another few weeks. But we're hopeful."

"Well," Mr. Tobey added, "you're doing a good thing, caring for him. And let's hope he's a survivor like his son."

He stepped back slightly and smiled at the group of men. "It was good to reconnect with you all," he pronounced, as if addressing a large audience. "I'm going to have a moment up front with George, and then go find Stephen and Margaret. Take care." With that, he turned and walked away.

A moment later, a man in a dark suit ushered everyone toward the folding chairs that filled the main room. Mike and the others took their seats toward the back, mostly in an effort to make sure the family was able to sit toward the front, but it had the added benefit of placing them a bit farther away from Daniel Tobey. The funeral service was short and simple, though sadness was heavy in the air. Within thirty minutes it was over.

"I don't know about you guys," Roger said quietly as the five friends stood up, "but I could sure as hell use a drink. Let's get out of this place."

No one protested.

* * *

Though it was out of the way for Mike, Hank, and Steve, the drive to Salem had been worth it. The Filthy Pig was a rustic, hole-in-the-wall sort of place where it felt perpetually dark inside, even with the window shades thrown wide. Dark wood, dim lights, and the smallness of the space all conspired to create intimacy and solitude. It was the perfect spot for five grieving friends to gather and reflect.

The Filthy Pig was laid out in the shape of the letter 'U'. Upon entering, the main bar stared down at you from the opposite end of the room, and to its left was a small door that led into the dining area. They had arrived around 1:30 p.m. and found a large booth along the wall across from that doorway.

Steve ordered a Bass ale. He always ordered a Bass, no matter where he was, variety be damned. Mike, Hank and Bill each got a glass of the seasonal on tap, a dark brew with a healthy head of foam and a sweet, roasted scent. Roger, being Roger, ordered a whiskey.

"Starting hard right out the gate, eh man?" Hank mentioned to his friend.

"Beer then liquor, get drunk quicker," Roger recited. "Liquor then beer, you're in the clear." He grinned at the off-duty detective beside him. Hank deadpanned for a moment and then smiled back.

Bill shifted in his seat and pulled a small notebook and pen out of his back pocket. "I don't think I've ever heard that one before," he said to Roger. "It would make a perfect addition to a future book, though." Bill smiled weakly.

"I'll tell you what would make a great novel," Roger replied, his judgment as slurred as his speech. "That crazy story about George would, right? I mean, come on. A message in blood?"

Steve winced at Roger's lack of tact. "Come on man, George was a friend."

"Think I don't know that?" Roger bit back. He wasn't an angry drunk—more of the fall-on-his-ass-laughing kind of drunk—but he seemed genuinely serious this time. "But that's not natural, man. Something happened to George and that scares the piss out of me."

"I think I'm going to do some poking around tomorrow," said Hank. "It's not my case, but maybe Gloucester will be willing to share some information me. I know someone on the force over there, and he might be able to help me out."

Mike nodded. "Good idea. I understand if you can't share what you learn, but it would be a relief to know at least one of us has a clue about what happened."

"I've lived in Hollesley for thirty-five years and I don't think I've ever heard of this area he was hiking in," said Steve. "Granted, I spend most of my days either working or managing two crazy little kids, but still, how odd."

"No, you've been to there before, Steve," said Bill. "You just don't remember it."

As a writer living in Salem, of course he knew more than a little about it. It was part of the overall mythos of the region, a stone in the supernatural wall that seemed to surround most of Cape Ann. But Bill first learned about it the same way the rest of the gang did.

Steve looked confused. "What are you talking about, man?"

"Dogtown? September of 1991?" Bill asked, looking for recognition in his friend's eyes. "It was right before the school year started. We all spent an afternoon there. You don't remember?"

"Wait," said Hank. "You mean, that place we all ran around in the woods, with the rocks and small pits? Man, I forgot all about that."

Bill could see recognition dawn on everyone's face. "You guys just didn't know that place was called Dogtown back then. I didn't either, but I've learned about Dogtown since, enough that I was able to make the connection."

They had begged their parents for months to go hiking somewhere. It was the kind of summer that seemed to be missing the excitement and adventure of their childhood, and maybe they had just wanted to try and rekindle it. An expedition into the woods, they thought, would be just the thing.

It had been hard to find a time when all seven of them were around at the same time. Summers were filled with family vacations and trips to Singing Beach. Hank was gone most of June with his family on their road trip to the Grand Canyon and Yellowstone. Bill himself, the group's only Boy Scout and the one who had come up with the idea in the first place, was gone with his parents for two weeks at the end of July, traveling up the coast of Maine to Prince Edward Island and back.

Finally, toward the end of August, the seven boys were able to get their families to agree on a Saturday in early September. The seven boys piled into the back of Mr. Tobey's 1981 Ford Bronco and took the short drive up Route 128 to Grant Circle and 127. It had rained that morning and the trees were still damp, but the area was quiet and beautiful. Kenny's father stayed in the truck, having brought along a dog-eared copy of some Louis L'Amour novel to read while he waited.

They did the usual things that any visitor to Dogtown can still do today, walking the trails and locating the foundations and sunken cellars of the old homes that once stood around the Commons. Of course, a group of unmonitored boys were apt to attempt things that modern hikers wouldn't necessarily consider, let alone attempt, such as scaling some of the larger boulders that dotted the old settlement.

Some of them were as large as a house. One such boulder was known as the Whale's Jaw. It once resembled the head of a whale breaking through the ground to reach upward, mouth agape, but in 1989 some irresponsible hikers allowed a campfire to get out of control and the natural arrangement was forever altered. That didn't stop Kenny and Hank from trying to climb it, though.

The others might have forgotten their trip to Dogtown, but Bill felt uncomfortable every time he thought back to that afternoon. He remembered standing with his back to the forest of trees that had overgrown the old settlement, watching Kenny scale the curved side of the Whale's Jaw while Hank stood atop, cheering him on and offering comparisons of the smaller boy's performance to long-dead relatives. Mike, Roger and Steve were still exploring the old town square, little more than a small grassy clearing surrounded by trees now, hoping to find some artifact or relic in the dirt. George, being as close to a second shadow Kenny might ever have had, was standing below his friend, arms held up, ready to catch him if he fell.

It struck Bill how unnaturally quiet it was. Here they were, in the center of busy Cape Ann, a short distance from the busy 128 and directly beneath one of Logan Airport's busy flight paths, and he was certain he could still hear the grass move in the wind. It was in that silence that he heard a twig snap somewhere in the brush behind him.

He still wasn't sure what he had seen that day. He remembered turning around and noticing how deep some of the shadows were in the thick of the trees and shrubs that filled the border of the site. There was the slightest flicker of movement in there, but what had it been?

The quills. That's all he remembered.

There had been something, maybe just some stray branches moving in the wind. Bill saw them for the briefest of moments before they vanished behind a tree. *They're just sticks, moving with the wind*, he remembered thinking. But they never moved back into view.

What was odd about them was how uniform they were. Long and slender, pale and natural like a piece of unfinished wood. There were as many as a dozen, all clustered together about shoulder height — though at thirteen his shoulders weren't more than four and a half feet off the ground. It was how orderly they looked that troubled him the most, though, as if they had grown together.

Years later, while studying for a college ecology course, Bill had happened across a photo of a porcupine and his eyes froze on the quills that protruded from the back of the animal. Pale and orderly, long and slender, they seemed to be a ghostly echo of a childhood memory.

"Bill?" It was Mike, and his hand was on Bill's wrist. "You all right, man? We lost you for a moment there."

Bill forced a smile. "Yeah," he said unconvincingly. "I'm good."

"I can't believe I forgot about that day in the woods," Hank continued. "I climbed that huge boulder, didn't I?"

"The Whale's Jaw," Mike muttered. "Yeah, that was it. You and Kenny, I think."

Bill nodded. He remembered it clearly. Too clearly.

CHAPTER FOUR

The group ended their time at the pub when Steve realized, in something of a panic, that he needed to get home in roughly three minutes for dinner with his family. That broke the mood and sent the rest of the men reaching for their coats, though much more slowly than the tardy family man.

Steve and Hank left with Mike, who gave them a ride back to the funeral home where they had each left their cars. Roger mentioned walking, but Bill quickly offered to give him a lift back to his apartment. It was out of the way for Bill, and that was no small sacrifice in the October version of Salem, but that's what friends were for. Roger was also the most inebriated of the bunch, and Bill had a nasty feeling that, even walking, his friend was going to have a hard time making it home safely.

Roger rented a small one-bedroom apartment near the corner of Derby and Turner, close to the water and the famed Turner House. No one actually called it that, though. Instead, the house had inherited the title bestowed upon it in the mid-nineteenth century by a

Nathaniel Hawthorne novel. Fiction had now become reality, and the sprawling, black-sided structure was forevermore known as the House of the Seven Gables.

Not that Roger paid attention to things like that. No, that was a detail that fell within the realm of William J. McCarthy, best-selling author and amateur historian extraordinaire. Roger was more concerned with earning enough cash to buy another cheap bottle of Smirnoff or Jack than he was with the history of his neighborhood. Amazingly though, with the right motivation, even he could be a hard worker.

Roger had worked as a house painter for over a decade, working on the crew of one of the larger companies in the Cape Ann area. Even when he wasn't working it was common to find him wearing paint-stained white denim and a pale gray sweatshirt. He worked hard, knew his trade well, and never came to work drunk, though he was frequently hungover and blood-shot from the previous evening's conversation with the bottle.

His apartment was one of two units on the third floor over a retail space that turned over business tenants as frequently as the seasons. A year ago it had been a high-end children's maternity store, *Baby Bumps*, which closed and became a gourmet tea shop for a few months. Now it had become the home for one of the countless roast beef sandwich shops that were scattered across the region. At least the smell that drifted up through the vents was pleasant.

Bill located a parking space on the street and pulled in, his front right tire catching the curb and twisting the steering wheel slightly in his hands. The sun had begun its final descent and the sky was illuminated with yellows and pinks.

"All set, Roger," he said to his friend, who had been mostly silent for the duration of the drive over. Roger snorted and woke with a start.

"What? Where?" he muttered, looking around at his surroundings. "Oh man, you're the best," he slurred. "Next time I'll drive, I swear. I owe you, man."

Bill chuckled. "I'd never risk my life so flippantly," he replied. "I enjoy helping you out and it wasn't a bad drive. Nearly hit a couple of tourists, though."

"Screw 'em," Roger muttered again. "Damn flies, that's all they are. Flies looking for food on a dirty floor. Every damn year."

"They also bring their money into the city, remember?" Bill offered in the defense of the visitors. "Some of that money buys your drink. Don't forget that part." He smiled.

Roger spent many summer nights with his hat on the sidewalk and his lips on the saxophone, teasing the coins and small bills out of people's wallets with a skill that would have made the piper of Hamelin jealous. He wasn't the best sax player in the world, but he wasn't the worst either, and the tourists never could resist the urge to reward him with handfuls of coins.

"Let's get you upstairs, man," Bill said, opening his door. Roger fumbled at his own, but Bill beat him, helping the man to his feet. He pressed a finger to the door handle and the small *chirp* of the lock engaging echoed off the storefront beside them.

"Fancy," muttered Roger with a smirk.

"Perks of the job, buddy," he grinned back. "Got your keys?"

Roger reached into his pockets and brought out a small set of keys, handing them to Bill. Then they slowly made their way over to the dark doorway set in between *Eddie's Beef and Seafood* and the Vietnamese nail salon. Once inside, they mounted the stairs—carefully and slowly, of course—until Roger's door greeted them in the dim light of the third floor hallway.

"Thanks, Bill," Roger slurred, "I've got it from here."

He tried one key, and then another. Then he dropped them. Bill picked them up off the short, rough, age-old carpet and handed them back by the correct key, making sure Roger took notice.

Finally, the door opened on the dark apartment and Bill could smell the stench of weeks of binge drinking drift out into the hall. It smelled like a college dorm, a North End bar, and a trash can all at the same time, and Roger grinned as he staggered through the doorway.

"Home sweet home," he said, his voice sincere and cheerful.

"You're good, man?" Bill asked. *This must be what parents feel like when they drop their kids off at school*, he thought.

"I'm good," Roger slurred back, his voice failing to instill confidence. "Thanks for the ride, man. Watch out for the flies on your way home." The man flashed a drunk, comical grin.

"You bet. Take it easy, my friend," Bill replied, and then pulled the door closed and headed back down the stairs.

He glanced at his watch. *Only 6:15 p.m.* On a whim he walked past his car and headed toward Turner Street. Turning south, he made his way casually toward the parking lot and grounds that mark the outer border of the Turner House. The evening air was heavy with the scent of salt water and a cool breeze was gently moving the leaves overhead. If peace could have a sound, Bill was sure this was it.

The museum would be locked already, tours having ended fifteen minutes prior, but he knew that if he wandered farther down the street toward the ocean he would be able to access the green space that abutted the property. The evening had grown dark enough that he could easily see the station out at the end of Derby Wharf, and the sound of the water lapping against the stone breakwater near where the sidewalk ended.

Bill took a seat on a low wall that separated the yard from the street. There was a lot to process, and so much of it was unexpected. George's death had been shock enough when it had no narrative or reason, but knowing now what had been discovered he felt shaken.

Seeing Kenny's father had also been unexpected, and he had been forced to deal with emotions he hadn't been prepared to acknowledge just yet. He certainly didn't hold on to the level of guilt that Mike did, but that was out of the ordinary for most people.

Sure, Mike had led them into that old mill, but it had been Hank's idea originally. And even though he had been the de facto leader in the basement of the building, there was so much confusion in the rush to escape the room that it was impossible to blame one single person for Kenny's death. Mike was hardly innocent, but no one in the group could be considered guilty of murder.

Now George was dead. No one could take the blame for that, though. Mike may try to make it his fault —that man could use some serious time in a therapist's office, for sure—but George died far from all of them, without their involvement or knowledge. Guilt would be hard to come by, even for Mike.

Bill had to wonder if this could have come at a worse time, but quickly dismissed the thought. *Idiot*, he muttered to himself, *the unexpected is never convenient*. No, most people only had two options when tragedy landed in their laps: bitch and moan because it upset their carefully-laid plans, or find the reason and purpose in the moment.

He wasn't necessarily a religious man, though like most of the others he was raised in the local Catholic church. He understood how it worked for people that believed in God, but chose to work through it on his own terms. He wasn't looking for the divine in each moment, or questioning God's will or plan or whatever others called it. He was simply acknowledging the fact that, quite often, tragedies and unplanned circumstances acted much the same way an alarm clock does. Everyone needs a nudge to stay awake.

One thing he did know is that all of this unexpectedness was going to throw off his writing. Some of it, as pointed out by Kenny's father, had to do with new inspiration. Bill wasn't above using events and people from his real life as influences on the novels he wrote. When the subject matter fit so well into his typical choice for genre, all the better. Sometimes it was drawn directly from his own experiences, and sometimes from simple observation of others.

The opening sequence of his second novel, *The Dark Road*, was nearly a word-for-word description of a moment in his own life. In the story, a young man named James Hutchinson had been driving home from a wedding reception late at night after having dropped his date off in the neighboring town. A few miles from home, on a small road that cut through a patch of woodland, Hutchinson had seen a shape on the side of the road.

The novel detailed the events that transpired after the character pulled over and searched the foliage at the edge of the road for what he thought was an injured animal. What he discovered, though, was far from natural. And it was the perfect setup for what became a national bestseller and a major motion picture just sixteen months later.

Bill could still remember actually driving that road in the dark. It had been a book signing in Rockport that he was returning home from rather than the fictional reception, and there was no date to drop off, but he had indeed seen a shape that baffled and concerned him, and he did pull over. Every fiber in his being told him not to, but he did nonetheless.

He never did find an animal in those roadside bushes, dead or alive, though there were a few moments where he was certain he was being watched by whatever had crossed the road. He remembered how anthropomorphized that unseen creature had become in his mind's eye, verging something close to human. He had never been sure why he felt that way—perhaps it was just the overactive imagination of a writer of fiction—but he could never shake it. So he put it into a novel instead.

It had become a sort of therapy for him, actually. While Bill McCarthy was loath to enter into confrontation in person, he found he was able to work his complaints and critical observations into the words he wrote on the page. By changing the names and descriptions that inspired him to something benign, he found a new freedom. Life was generous, too, and it usually offered more inspiration than he could typically fit into his novels. He wasn't about to complain; he was just happy to have that material to draw upon.

Bill stood up and took one last look at the dark waters of the ocean and the dots of light that were scattered around the wharf before walking back up Turner Street toward his car. He had no family to get home to like Steve did, but his work awaited him like an anxious spouse, and he was hoping to spend some quality time with her tonight.

His dilemma now was found in the source of this new inspiration. George had been more than a mere acquaintance; he had been a childhood friend who experienced real tragedy at Bill's side, and they had both carried their guilt and pain—mostly in silence, but sometimes in conversation—for two decades. Dipping into this emotional well, however appropriate for the type of novel Bill preferred to write, felt wrong. Not in the same way that shoplifting was wrong, but more akin to the way incest violates a definitive moral imperative. Writing about George would be tantamount to selling his own soul.

Now, with his current novel stalled and his editor at Lawton and Dunning breathing down his neck, inspiration was precisely what Bill needed. Only he couldn't use this one. It was as if he had engaged a sort of moral parking break on his writing, and he was incapable of moving forward, despite the engine running hot and loud.

Jean Michaud, his editor, was about as tightly wound as they come. Bill would never say anything to her about that little observation, of course, but he *had* managed to work the conversation he dreamed of having into his most recent novel. He still smiled each time he recalled crafting that scene, and the clever dialogue she and another character traded regarding her ability to eat coal and crap diamonds.

The real-life tightwad, Jean, held Bill to deadlines like a mortgage company, and emailed weekly for status updates on whatever project happened to be in the works at the time. She called nearly as frequently, and even those conversations grew more frequent closer to a deadline. It was the perfect vaccination against creativity, though non-confrontational Bill McCarthy could never tell her that.

He slid into his car and pressed the button beside the shifter, gently nudging the engine to life. He would be home in less than ten minutes, at his desk within fifteen, and frustrated to the point of insanity within forty-five. He may not be an alcoholic like Roger, but he was glad for the unopened bottle of Glenlivet Single Malt he had waiting for him in the cabinet beside his writing desk.

The drive across town from the wharf area to his home in the Chestnut Street District was short and uneventful. The number of tourists had thinned out from their peak at midday, making for less frequent stops at crosswalks and traffic lights. Bill was anxious for October to be over, at which point life in the city would get back to normal.

If things can get back to normal, that is, he thought to himself.

Bill's neighborhood was also known as the McIntire Historic District, named after the famous American architect, Samuel McIntire, who lived and worked in Salem near the end of the Eighteenth century. The buildings that he designed and built were strong, linear, and simple, and many still stand to this day.

He remembered reading somewhere that Chestnut Street was considered one of the most beautiful neighborhoods in America, and it was difficult to believe otherwise. Bill's home was just around the corner from the old Hamilton Hall, a historic meeting space with one of the first sprung dance floors in the country, supposedly designed by Benjamin Franklin himself.

A narrow cobblestone drive ran down the right side of the large red brick house and ended at a small garage large enough to hold Bill's car and a few lawn implements. The motion light affixed to the rear corner of the house flicked on as he slowly pulled down the drive, and he reached up to press the button on his door opener.

The light inside the garage came on, but the door did not rise. He pressed the button again, but the result was the same as before.

"Great," he said aloud to himself. "That caps a fantastic day, for sure."

Bill had been aware that the garage door mechanism was old when he purchased the house and that a replacement was needed sooner rather than later, but had never managed to find the time to get it taken care of. It seemed that whatever final thread had been holding up the functionality of the door had finally snapped.

He shifted the car into park and killed the engine. Leaving it outside wouldn't be his preference, but it seemed that tonight he was without alternatives. And since tomorrow was Sunday, it would be at least another night before a company would be able to come out and replace the broken system.

Ever a lover of order and patterns, Bill could feel himself growing frustrated as he climbed out of the car and locked the door. On a whim he approached the garage and tried to manually raise the door, but it refused to budge. With a sigh, he turned and crossed the driveway, making his way toward the small span of black iron fence that connected the garage to the house, and opened the gate in the center.

The back yard was a study in light and shadow. The motion light was powerful, and even though it pointed toward the driveway, enough light spilled out into the rear yard to expose most of the property. Deep shadows spread out from the corners of the yard, reaching into the lit areas like fingers.

A few steps from the back door, the motion light flickered slightly. At the same moment, Bill heard a rustling from the far edges of the yard, just out of the reach of his vision.

Vader, he thought. His neighbors to the left had a spunky black lab that they called Vader, and it was common to find him wandering through the back yard after having jumped over the low iron fence. There were more trees in the rear of Bill's property than his neighbor's and Vader loved to explore and mark his territory.

Seeing as he didn't have a dog of his own, Bill allowed this, but only reluctantly. Vader had a tendency to leave piles of feces and the occasional dead squirrel on his lawn, something that disgusted Bill's obsessive-compulsive nature.

"Vader?" he called out, turning toward the trees across the yard. "Hey, boy, come on out." He couldn't remember the last time Peter and Sue had allowed Vader to wander over this late at night. "Here, boy!" he called out again.

Bill stepped off the small brick walkway and into the grass. He kept his eyes on the lawn, watching his feet as he crossed the yard so he could avoid any of the presents the dog might have left for him. Stepping on a pile of dog crap might not be the ideal way to end such an exhausting day.

In the center of the yard he encountered his latest gardening project, a small raised bed for vegetables constructed of reclaimed timber. It was small, no larger than a couple feet on either side, but he had already begun to fill it with soil, and the two remaining bags lay beside it. His mother's copper hand trowel sat atop the pile.

He approached the edge of the shadows and ducked under a low branch from the oak that marked the end of the lawn. His feet crunched beneath him, passing from the soft grass into the thick layer of mulch that made up the ground-cover under the tree. Past the thick trunk of the tree was a cluster of low bushes and ornamental grass. Bill stepped up to the space between two of the shrubs and parted their leaves with both arms.

He saw black fur and relaxed. "There you are," he said cordially. "Come on out, boy. Time to go home."

But the shape did not respond. That wasn't strange; Vader was one of those dogs that could get so distracted that he would fail to hear a car honk if it was bearing down on him. No, the strange thing was how Vader didn't move at all. Not even the signs of breathing were evident.

Bill stepped forward, assuming he needed to draw the dog's attention away from whatever had captivated it in the undergrowth. He leaned down and pushed more of the shrub aside, and then immediately fell backward to land in the mulch and dirt on his rear.

He tried to scream, but all that exited his mouth was a hoarse rasp. What he had seen in the bushes had sent his heart tumbling into the pit of his stomach. Vader was there on his side, covered by the short branches and green leaves, but his head was gone. A large patch that looked black in the shadows had surrounded the dog's body like a glistening pool of darkness, and Bill knew instinctively that it was blood. The strong scent of copper that hung in the air confirmed that assumption.

He turned to run back toward the house but his legs refused to cooperate. They felt numb and powerless.

His head. The dog's head was gone. Why? What? His mind raced through a litany of questions and he cried out in fear. He didn't have time to think beyond that, but before he could move, the motion light near the driveway turned off completely, leaving him in the dark.

The fear was now propelling him away from the bushes. He clawed at the mulch and soil in an attempt to move faster, but his damned legs were still refusing to work.

Had he really seen what he thought he had? The dog's head had been gone, yes, but there had been eyes. Not Vader's eyes. No, these were smaller, more bright and menacing. Was something else in the brush? A wild animal? He thought...no...surely he had imagined that. Hadn't he?

Bill glanced back. He was lying on the edge of the grass now, where the chaos and filth of the mulch gave way to the orderly lawn. He looked over his side at the bushes where he found the dog and saw them moved.

"Help!" he cried out and turned back toward the house. He regained his knees this time, pulling one heavy leg beneath him, and then another. Over and over he repeated this, churning forward.

One more glance backward showed him the same movement. Perhaps it was the wind. Or perhaps whatever it was that had ripped off the dog's head was now moving to chase him. Regardless, Bill didn't want to stick around to find out. He lunged toward the house.

It wasn't the headless dog that drove him forward. It wasn't the red eyes he had glimpsed in the darkness. It was something else, something that cut deep into his memories like a long, cruel knife blade. It was what he saw around the dog's neck, like a hideous collar, before the light had gone out.

Quills.

There had been long, pale quills protruding from the dog's neck. Dozens of them. Bent askew and bristling outward in imitation of some twisted cactus.

Quills. Bill moaned at the thought. *Oh god, the quills.*

As if the thought had propelled him forward, he finally found his feet. He threw himself into a run. To an outsider it might have appeared a drunken run, or the gait of someone badly injured. If Bill was drunk with anything, though, it was fear.

He forced himself to look one last time toward the back of the yard. They were there again: red eyes. He hadn't been imagining it. The back of the yard was washed in deep shadows, but he could see them starring at him, as if they were studying him.

The eyes were unearthly. They were farther off the ground than one might have expected for an animal— perhaps three feet, maybe more—and they were burning, too. They were small and vicious, glaring out at him from the darkness.

Suddenly there was a shrill hiss and Bill felt his testicles retreat into his body. Then the bushes erupted as whatever it was inside them burst forth toward him. Bill cried out in horror and turned to run, tripping over his own feet in the process. Here he was, no more than ten feet from the back door of his own home, and yet he feared that he wasn't going to make it.

It was the stack of unused potting spoil that tripped him, though. He caught his shin on one of the soft yet immovable packages and went sprawling onto the grass. As he hit the ground, he felt a small shape land on his lower back and buttocks.

It reminded him of visits to his sister's house. Kate and her husband Rob had three small children, all boys, who were quite the handful. Their oldest, Malcolm, was six, and he loved to wrestle with Bill when he visited. Malcolm's preferred method of wrestling involved jumping off of the couch onto Bill's back.

It was that feeling—the sensation of a small body landing on his back—that he was reminded of as the animal, or whatever it was, connected with his exposed backside. He couldn't see it, but he could feel that same panic people do when a spider falls from the ceiling and disappears into their clothing. He twisted and lurched, doing everything he could to dislodge it.

In the process of writhing, Bill's hand landed on the copper hand trowel. He grasped it as tight as he could in his left hand, and then swung that arm backward toward his backside. The animal hissed once more when it saw the attack coming, and then Bill felt the sharp edge of the trowel collided with furry flesh and the bone beneath. Injured, the animal toppled off his back and into the grass.

Bill wasted no time. He sprung to his feet and bolted toward the house. His keys were out in seconds and he practically slammed into the space beside to the door. He fumbled with the few keys on the ring until he found the house key, and then shoved it into the lock as fast as he could manage.

The tumbler shifted, the knob turned, and he spilled into the back entry, tripping over a pair of gardening shoes. *The door*, his mind screamed in a panic, and he scrambled to his feet and pushed the door closed. Bill twisted the small lock on the nob and then turned the deadbolt before he peered out through the small window.

For a moment he expected to see the animal standing there, glaring at him again, but it was gone. Bill wasn't sure, but he thought he saw a thin wisp of smoke over the spot of the lawn where he had been tackled. Whatever it had been, though, the animal had vanished.

Bill slumped with his back against the locked door and grasped at his knees. He was shaking and panting with exertion and filled with adrenaline, and he didn't want to move. He felt no pain, but he could still feel the weight of that...that thing...on his back.

Then he remembered the quills and began to scream.

CHAPTER FIVE

Every evening for Steve Bowers followed the same predictable pattern. Predictable and comforting, really. A lesser parent would complain about the monotony of it all, how every day was the same without variation and the days and weeks seemed to blur into one long waking dream. But Steve was one of those parents who loved the small moments and knew that the early years of parenthood would give way to chaos soon enough. He wanted to enjoy every moment that he could.

Steve managed to make it home from the Filthy Pig just as his wife Beth was setting out dinner. Dinner was late, thankfully, which helped him escape her ire as best as he could. The smell of beer on his breath wasn't helping, though.

Dinner for he and Beth was served on the same stoneware plates they had used since they were married nine years before. The girls, though, ate off small plastic plates that looked more like frisbees than dinnerware. They were indestructible, brightly colored, and dishwasher safe, which made them a parent's dream.

When he walked in the door, Molly, the older of the two girls at five, was already perched atop her booster seat at the table. Her younger sister, Sarah, still used a highchair and was buckled in and tugging at her bib.

"How was it?" Beth asked from her seat at the table. Steve passed behind her and leaned down to kiss her on the head. Moving to his side of the table, he tickled each girl on the side of the neck as he passed them, and then took up his normal station across from his wife.

"It was tough," he said with a flat tone. "It was good to have all the guys together again, but man, I wished it was under better circumstances."

Beth nodded. "Molly, lean over your plate," she said firmly. "I told you that at breakfast, too. I want the food to fall on your plate, not your shirt." Molly scooted herself in slightly, and made a nominal effort to lean over the plate on her next bite. Sarah's water bottle fell from the highchair and crashed on the floor.

"How were Stephen and Maggie?" she asked Steve as she leaned over to retrieve the bottle. Though Beth hadn't grown up with any of the others from Steve's childhood, she knew Margaret Ashcroft from the local food bank where Beth volunteered once a week. Stephen Ashcroft was on the food bank's board, and Maggie was behind the counter every morning without fail. "It was such a shock for all of us there. I can't imagine what she's going through right now."

Steve nodded. It was hard to say more in front of the kids.

"Who's going through what?" Molly asked innocently while trying to spear a piece of chicken with her fork.

Beth smiled. "Just someone we know, sweetie. They've lost someone very close to them, and it's made them sad. It's made a lot of people sad."

Molly mopped up a glob of ketchup with the chicken and pushed the whole mess into her mouth. "Whu da dey lus im?" She managed to say.

Steve chuckled. It felt good to laugh after a day so full of sadness. "You won't believe me if I tell you this, Molly, but I didn't understand a thing you just said." She grinned at him, her eyes squinted and head tilted sideways. "Try it again after you've swallowed that bite."

After another moment of herculean chewing, she said it again. "Where did they lose him?"

Beth's face seemed to be caught between laughter and tears. "Oh sweetie," she said, but trailed off. Sarah tossed her balled-up napkin onto the table and it rolled across Beth's plate and off onto the floor.

"Sarah," Steve groaned. "Are you allowed to throw things?"

"No," she replied in a voice that was far too cute for her own good.

"No, you aren't," he added firmly. "Don't do it again, all right?"

"M-hm," she mumbled around a bite of food.

Dinner progressed this way for another thirty minutes through the main course and the successive rounds of what Molly liked to call *something else*, as in, "Can I have something else?"

After everything was cleaned up and the girls were wiped clean, the last phase of the evening commenced. That hour between dinner and the time when the girls went to bed was like the last mile of a marathon. For Beth, it was the end of another day of keeping the kids constantly active, engaged and occupied. For Steve, it was an exercise in managing chaos, something that was worse after dinner because he was exhausted and the kids were energized from their meal.

While Beth cleaned off the dishes and loaded them into the dishwasher, Steve was building the largest blanket fort in all of the North Shore. A series of walls had been constructed with cushions from the couch and the big armchair, and a blanket had been slung over a pair of dinner room chairs and secured with some handy clamps. The space inside might be too snug for Steve to crawl through comfortably, but the girls were in heaven.

"Turn off all the lights, daddy," Molly begged from somewhere in the bowels of the cloth and cushion fortress. "Make it dark!"

Steve chuckled and flicked off the lights in the room and the adjoining hallway. This had become the new obsession for the girls. Molly clearly enjoyed it more than Sarah who still struggled with the fear of the dark that most three-year old kids do. She put on a brave face, but frequently ended up in the kitchen hugging Beth's legs.

This time she had crawled deep inside the fort. Steve lowered himself to his belly and squirmed his head and shoulders through one of the openings. There was a faint light inside, and at first he couldn't figure out why. Then he realized that Sarah was holding a small flashlight, and the batteries were losing strength, giving the light a weak, blueish glow.

"Does that help, sweetie?" he asked with a grin, hoping to keep the little girl cheerful. Sarah responded by pointing the light at his face and saying something that sounded like *sparkly tights,* but he wasn't sure.

"What's that, honey?"

"Sparkly lights," she said more clearly. "Like in the backyard. Lights that float. Pretty lights."

Steve nodded. He wasn't sure what she was talking about. The season for lightening bugs was well over, and even in the summer they had been hard to find. She couldn't have meant headlights from cars because their backyard abutted a small wetland area and there were no roads on the other side of it that he was aware of.

"What lights, honey?" he squirmed a bit farther in to be closer to her. Molly had exited the fort on a different side and he could now hear her scaling the couch and digging for something on the other side of the blanket.

Sarah frowned and turned off the light. "I want mommy," she said with a whine, and then pushed Steve aside to crawl out and away. *Oh well*, he thought. *The Mystery of the Lights will have to wait, Sherlock.* He backed up and exited the fort, looking for whatever trouble Molly was getting into.

When he discovered that Molly had joined Sarah and Beth in the bathroom to have their teeth brushed, Steve set about cleaning up. There were days when the house looked as if a cyclone had torn through the living room, and other days when the girls managed to maintain some semblance of order and cleanliness. Today, unfortunately, was a day that fell into the former category.

The girls returned, running and screaming with laughter, as he was dropping the last of the pillows onto the large chair in the corner. Molly requested another fort and made a grab for a couch cushion, but Steve shut her down just as quickly.

"It's time to get calm, girls," he said loudly over their squeals and giggles. Sarah had become fascinated lately with her bum, and kept bending over and pulling her pants and diaper low enough for her older sister to see her tiny little cheeks. Molly giggled and Steve fought the urge to laugh as well.

Bedtime preparations went smoothly, and once each girl was comfortably sporting a pair of warm pajamas—the kind with the footsies built in, and a hood for chilly nights—they began the march upstairs to the girls' bedroom.

After reading a story about a little duck that was adamant about wanting boots, and a small fight over who got a larger sip of water from the cup, the girls were tucked in. Beth made sure Sarah was snug in bed, while Steve took care of Molly, and the light was turned off. Steve knelt down to kiss his oldest daughter one last time when she whispered up to him in the dim light.

"Tomorrow, I want to build the biggest fort ever, daddy," she said with a grin. "More bigger than the one we made today. Bigger than a house."

Steve smiled. "I'll have to call in a building inspector, then." He tapped the watch on his wrist and added, "Will you be able to wait till after breakfast for them to come over and give us the go-ahead?"

She nodded. Then a look of utter seriousness came over her face. "Daddy, I don't want the monsters to play in the fort, okay?"

Steve nodded, "Of course, sweetie. I'm not sure the fort will be big enough for monsters anyway. They're, what, like seventeen feet tall, right?"

Beth exited the room behind him and he was more than eager to join her in beginning the kidless portion of the evening, so he straightened up and got ready to stand. Molly wasn't satisfied, though.

"No daddy, the monsters are small," her little face turned a bit toward the middle of the room and her eyes rolled toward the floor. "They live under my bed. That's not a big place."

Steve pretended to peek under the covers and bed frame at the floor and then offered her a big smile. "All clear, sweetie," he said. "No monsters here. Or in the fort." He kissed her on the nose and stood up.

"I love you, Molly," he said. "I'll see you in the morning."

"I love you, daddy." Her little face smiled back at him from within the tangle of pajamas and blankets, and Steve turned and stepped out of the room, quietly pulling the door closed behind him.

With his back turned, he wasn't able to see the shadow that moved under the bed, or the faint light that glistened off something wet and round. Something that might have been an eye.

* * *

Mike Barton washed off the single plate that he had used for his dinner, a sparse meal that consisted of a microwavable chicken potpie and some sweet potato chips that he found in the pantry. Like most meals, Mike ate this one on the couch while watching the television, usually one of the half-dozen or so singing competition programs that filled the prime time schedule.

He could remember how, just a few years ago, there had been only one show that pitted amateur singers against each other in pursuit of a lofty prize, but the concept—and the potentially explosive marketing machine that followed it—had caught like wildfire, and now each major network had one or two similar shows in their lineup. If you had seen one celebrity judge throw a tantrum, Mike thought, you had seen them all.

That didn't stop him from regularly watching one or two of these shows, however, and he was fairly convinced that the skinny girl with the red hair and the Janis Joplin pipes was going to win the show on NBC. *Damn, she can sing.* It was like listening to her soul. She dug deep and really put herself into her performances. It was amazing to see.

Tonight, though, he had little desire to escape into television. He managed to watch the first fifteen minutes of the program before he switched it off and finished his meal while staring vacantly at the glossy black rectangle that hung on the wall. Now he stood in the kitchen at the sink, washing away the crumbs from his meal. *If only it were this easy to wash away mistakes*, he thought. *I'd probably need a bigger sink, though.*

Even before they transpired, he had expected the events of today to test his emotional limits, and they had done just that. With the exception of Bill, he had fallen out of regular contact with the rest of the old gang. Sure, he saw Hank around town from time to time, enough to be able to skip that whole '*Wow, it's been such a long time. How've you been?*' conversation. He wasn't getting together for drinks with him like he did with Bill, though.

Roger and Steve were almost like strangers. They had lives that rarely overlapped with Mike's, and even though he missed the camaraderie of his childhood, he was mostly glad for the distance between them now. After all, the more he saw his old friends, the more he had to think about Kenny. And that was something Mike tried to avoid at all costs.

Ultimately, he knew that it was his fault that he wasn't closer with the rest of them. He threw himself into his job, and was a textbook example of a workaholic. He barely had time for himself, let alone old friends.

Mike was drying off the dish he had used and was reaching into the cupboard to place it back on the small stack inside when he heard a knock at the door. The knock was fast and hard, not the typical post-dinner rapping that bordered on polite gentleness. It was the kind of knock that caused a person's heart to stutter and then race.

What the hell? Who in the world would be looking for me at this hour? He glanced at the digital clock on the microwave over the stove. The small green numbers told him it was nearly 11 p.m. The knock came again, more urgent this time. *Seriously, what the hell?*

He closed the cupboard and passed through the wide archway that separated the kitchen and the dinning room, and then into the front hallway. He pushed aside the white sheer that hung across the small window at the top of the door and glanced outside.

It was Bill, and he was standing on Mike's front porch, glancing erratically around. Mike jerked the door open.

"Bill?" he asked with concern. "What the hell is wrong, man?"

His friend pushed past him and into the house. Mike stepped back to let him through and then pulled the door shut.

"Bill..." he started again, but his friend interrupted him.

"I was attacked in my back yard," he said. His face was painted with panic and fear, and he couldn't seem to take his eyes off the window in the dinning room. "Something...an animal...I don't know. And my neighbor's dog...oh Mike. The dog's head was gone!"

"Whoa, whoa, slow down," Mike said, opening his hands in a calming gesture. "Slow down and walk me through what happened." And then, following Bill's eyes once more to the window, "You're safe here. I'm not letting anyone else in, trust me."

He managed to guide Bill into the living room and get him seated on the couch. Mike sat in the armchair and leaned forward, elbows on his knees. "Talk, Bill," he said. His voice was calm and strong. "Tell me what happened."

The clock on the mantle had just sounded the small two-note chime that marked midnight by the time Bill slumped back into the couch, his story finally told. Mike could understand why his friend was as pale as a ghost and frightened out of his mind. What had happened, well, it would have scared the crap out of him as well.

"And you never got a good look at it?" he asked again, as if this time he might get an answer that was different. "Nothing but those small red eyes?"

Bill shook his head. "Nope." He looked down as he spoke, his eyes seeming to scan the carpet for an answer. "I ran, Mike. I wanted to be as far away from whatever it was, and as fast as possible."

He slowly shook his head from side to side. Mike thought he looked exhausted, and after everything that he and his friends had been through today, he imagined this was the last straw for Bill. His friend looked drained.

"I've heard stories," Bill said, "of people who were attacked in the woods by wild animals. Rabid raccoons, defensive female squirrels, even territorial birds. Christ, I've even written about it in one of my books. I've always understood that an animal attack can be an utterly frightening experience. But I'll tell you, nothing could have prepared me for this. Nothing."

Mike nodded. "I remember, a few years ago, I went hiking with a girl I was dating. I think it was Susan," he paused, trying to remember if it had been her or Angela. "Whatever, that doesn't matter which one it was. Anyway, we were hiking out at Bradley Palmer State Park, over in Topsfield. And about an hour into our walk—and these aren't even crazy wild woods, mind you—we ran into a doe drinking out of a small brook."

He opened his hands and shrugged at the thought. "We were stupid, I know. But seeing something that wild, that out of the ordinary from our typical city life, we stopped and watched it. I think Susan even tried to pull her phone out to take a photo. Hell, maybe that was what caught the deer's eye. Because all of a sudden, that bitch whirled around and glared at us."

Bill's eyes were widening. A small piece of the panic that he had felt in his back yard was creeping back. "What did you do?"

"We ran," chuckled Mike, laughing at the memory. "God, we ran, and as fast as we could, too. I don't know what set it off. My guess is that it had a baby nearby in the bushes. Who knows. But I'll tell you, I pissed myself. I didn't tell the girl, of course—I've got a reputation to keep, you know—but I pissed enough to wet the front of my underwear. And we ran like the wind."

Bill smiled, but his expression sobered quickly.

"I guess I'm telling you this because I know what you mean. And not in the sympathetic *I want to sound like I've been in the same boat so that you feel comforted* sense. I really know what you're feeling. That fear can be..." he trailed off. "It's paralyzing, isn't it?"

Bill nodded. "Yep."

There was silence for a moment. Mike was letting the memory of that day in the woods wash over his mind again, looking for some hope or piece of advice to offer Bill, but his friend cut in before he could speak.

"What do you think it was?" Bill asked timidly. "I mean, I'm not exactly on the edge of town where I live. What kind of wild animal roams that far into a city like Salem?"

"I heard once about a moose that wandered into downtown Lowell, man. That's a city of over eighty-thousand people, a veritable urban jungle. If a moose can do that, I think anything is possible." He smiled and leaned forward again. "My best guess? You had a visit from a coyote. I can't think of something else that would be as violent to a neighborhood pet."

Bill nodded, considering the idea. "A coyote?"

"Yup. It happens, man. Random, sure, and scary as hell. But it happens. Did you know Massachusetts, for all the millions of people in the Boston area and beyond, is about eighty percent woodland?"

"I think I've heard that, yeah," Bill nodded.

"We live in *their* territory, not the other way around," he concluded. "When things like this happen— my doe and your coyote—it's not because they've stepped out of their comfort zone and into our territory. No, it's because we're unwanted invaders, squatting in a place that's always belonged to them. We're in *their* way."

There was a moment when neither of them spoke. Bill seemed lost in thought, and Mike had leaned back in the chair and closed his eyes. He wasn't asleep, but he was quickly heading that way. It was Bill who once again broke the silence.

"Do you think I can stay here tonight?" His voice was polite but urgent. It was clear to Mike that his friend did not want to return home just yet.

"Absolutely," he responded. "Of course, you shouldn't expect me to make you breakfast in the morning. I save that treat for only the most special of ladies."

Both men grinned.

"What you should definitely do, though, is be sure to call Animal Control in the morning. They'll get right on it and maybe offer you some peace of mind. At the very least, they can help your neighbor move the body of their dog."

Bill agreed. He doubted that he would find any peace, no matter whom he called, but having someone else there to take care of the mess would be helpful. That was at least something. And after a day like this one, he wasn't about to be picky.

CHAPTER SIX

Hank Phillips wasn't a religious man by any stretch of the imagination. Though he grew up with parents who took him to St. Mary's downtown in Hollesley. They were far from regular attenders, though, and Hank had learned to associate church with holidays and funerals and nothing more. Most Sunday mornings felt just like any other morning of the week, especially when he had to work.

Today, for the first time in decades, he felt a strong desire to delay work and drop in on one of the small churches along High Street. Between the funeral and the afternoon of conversation with the others, he felt far from at peace. He felt that he needed to somehow hit the rest button on his mind and clear his system.

Rather than church, though, Hank headed toward Dogtown. He hoped that a bit of work might bring him focus. Work always took his mind off of his personal life. When his marriage fell apart a few years earlier, he had occupied himself with time at the office helping other detectives with difficult cases. It was into his work that he poured himself during the early days of his father's cancer treatment. Roger had his bottle; Hank was a man who self-medicated with work.

The time he had logged had eventually paid off in his professional life, at least. Shortly after the divorce, Hank moved from the Hollesley Police Department to the State Police, where he quickly earned the rank of Lieutenant, working out of the Danvers headquarters for Troop A. Then, two years ago, he had been appointed Detective Lieutenant.

His trip to Dogtown was far from official, but his position with the State Police would help regardless. His jurisdiction did not stop at the city line of Hollesley, and that access might be just what he needed to discover more about George's death — if not for the official investigation, then at least for himself.

Hank guided his unmarked Ford sedan up Route 128 toward Gloucester and Dogtown. He tried to set aside his personal misgivings about the details he knew of George's death, knowing he would need to be as objective as possible when he got there. His assistance might not have been requested, but he wanted to make sure that this intrusion could be as beneficial as possible should the Gloucester police get their panties in a bunch. The site would hopefully be unsupervised and empty, allowing him to move in and out without harassment.

After a short drive he turned into the gravel parking lot and got out of the car. He considered grabbing his coat, but the air was warmer than he had expected for a mid-October day. *Gotta love an Indian summer,* he thought.

He approached the large sign that welcomed him to *Historic Dogtown - Established 1641* and quickly found the trail he needed on the map. Armed with the map of the Babson Boulders that he had printed off the Internet earlier that morning, he set off at a brisk pace.

* * *

The boulder he was looking for rested near the railroad tracks, just north of the Babson Reservoir. It was set back off the path a bit, and stood among dozens of other smaller chucks of granite, the same type of stone that littered the earth across the entire area. The boulder he was looking for was easy to locate, having been surrounded with a bright band of yellow police tape.

It was larger than Hank had expected. As he approached, he sized it up and decided that it was at least a couple feet taller than him. The old Babson engraving of *SAVE* was carved into the face of the stone about belt-high in thick, angular letters.

The boulder also appeared to have a stone step extending from its base. It was on this step that Hank could see the remnants of the scene Stephen Ashcroft had told him about. The stone, though gray and mottled with green, was stained a dark color in the center of the step. A similar dark patch was smeared down the face of the boulder to the right of the carving. And below the large *SAVE*, Hank could see what was left of the chilling message, *YOURSELF*, written in sloppy letters in the same dark liquid that stained the base of the rock. It was illegible now, but he understood how powerful it must have been to see first-hand.

He tried to imagine the lettering before the elements of the last few days washed it away, and couldn't seem to make the shapes fit the words. There were five patches of darkness, with two directly below the engraving and then another three below that. Hank spent a few moments mentally forcing the word *YOURSELF* into those spaces, like a macabre jigsaw puzzle, but it didn't make sense. And then he figured it out: there had been four words, not one.

Whoever told Stephen Ashcroft that the entire message consisted of *YOURSELF* had censored the details. Whoever had written the message with George's blood on the face of the boulder had written five words. The

Gloucester police must have withheld those final words, though, and Hank wanted to know why.

Next he lifted the crime scene tape with one hand and slipped through. He studied what was left of George's blood on the step-like rock, and then glanced around the area, imagining how his friend's body might have lain broken in front of the boulder. The path was just far enough away to offer this location a bit of privacy, even during the daytime.

Looking at the large rock from the front, the best path into the forest beyond was to its left, where the leaf-covered ground slopped gently upward and into the woods. He stared at that area for a moment before finding what he was looking for.

Tracks.

They were faint but unmistakable, like dark lines carved into the soil of the hill. It looked like something— or some*one*—was dragged from the woods to the front of the boulder. Hank nodded as his experienced mind processed the details, building a more complete picture of what had happened.

He knew that it would have been risky for a killer to murder George in broad daylight, but it had happened nonetheless. His friend had come here in the morning, after sunrise, and was found before noon that same day, so an attack in darkness could be scratched off the list of options. That meant that whoever attacked George did so in a place that was far from visible.

He looked again at the boulder, and then past it into the woods. The trees there were younger and filled the space with their tall, narrow trunks. Even though some had already begun to drop their leaves, they would still have provided sufficient cover for anyone standing a few paces back from the rock.

There didn't seem to be any other option; George had been attacked in the woods before being dragged to the base of the *SAVE* boulder. There, his head was bashed against the stone step, most likely ending his life. The killer, whoever it was, then wrote their message under the engraving.

There was still the possibility that it had been George who wrote the message, as some form of warning perhaps. Hank had a difficult time believing that could be true, but decided that he would keep his mind open.

What about an accidental death? Could George have fallen here, maybe during an attempt to climb the boulder? Perhaps. The backside of the large stone did slope downward, giving it the appearance of a wedge from the side, making it easy to climb from behind.

Hank doubted that the fall would have been fatal from that height, though. No, from what George's father had said, and judging by the amount of blood that had stained these stones, this was much more than a hiking accident.

He stepped toward the marks in the dirt to the left of the boulder. Drag marks, surely. He followed them up the slight hill, careful to step around and not disturb the tracks in case the investigators from Gloucester needed to return and explore more for themselves. The marks stopped and started a number of times, reminding Hank of the dashed line down the center of the road. But this line led into the trees.

He had walked maybe a dozen feet before he stopped. Anyone coming from beyond this point would have had to move the low branches of the saplings aside to get through. Hank studied the slender limbs, looking for broken spots or torn leaves. Finally, he found something, but it was not what he had been expecting.

Down low, slightly higher than his knees, he found something hanging from one of the low leaves that still clung to the branch. A few somethings, actually. He knelt down and leaned forward to get a closer look. Then, reaching into his back pocket, he pulled out a white plastic envelope and a tool that resembled a small pair of tweezers.

He retrieved a sample of his discovery and carefully placed it into the envelope, which he then tucked away along with the tool. Hank stood back up and brushed off his knees, taking one last glance into the woods before heading back to the path. He had some thinking to do during his drive to Danvers.

* * *

Back at the car in the gravel parking lot, Hank pulled out his cell phone and dialed the number for the Gloucester Police Department. An operator answered the phone professionally, and he was quickly routed to the Detective Division.

After a few digital rings, a man with a gruff voice picked up the line and quickly barked a greeting.

"Lieutenant Kennedy," he said sharply. It was an ancient law enforcement technique, and Hank wasn't put off. Most officers answered public lines in the least welcoming manner possible, and for good reason.

In the early 1950's, a man had managed to have his call put through to the Detectives unit of the Boston city police department. The caller identified himself as a police Sergeant in Malden, wanting to pass along information relating to an ongoing investigation. The caller, it turned out, was the criminal at the center of the investigation.

While the information he gave to the Boston city officer later proved to be false, he managed to learn exactly what the investigation's next move would be, allowing him to alter his own plans accordingly.

Needless to say, the Boston city officer was reprimanded, and new policies were put in place to protect against future attempts at this kind of espionage. One such technique was to be as unfriendly as possible in the hopes that pranksters would be frightened off, something the man on the other end of the line was demonstrating now.

Thankfully, Hank knew Lieutenant Kennedy personally, and that gave him direct access that would have taken any other detective hours of cutting through red tape to obtain.

"Richard, it's Hank Phillips," he said calmly and then waited for the recognition.

"Well, I'll be," he replied. "Hank Phillips, how the hell are you?"

"I'm good, Richard, thanks. How's Barbara these days?"

"She's got me on a diet, Hank. A *diet*. Can you believe that?" Kennedy sounded incredulous, and Hank suppressed a laugh.

He could believe it, of course. Richard Kennedy was behind a desk for a reason; his days of active fieldwork were long behind him. At six feet tall and nearly two-eighty, he was a big boy, and the years—as well as his eating habits—had not been kind to his knees.

"You'll make it, Richard," he said with a smile. "You're a tough old boy, and I have a feeling that diet is going to crumble before you do."

The older officer laughed, and it sounded like a series of short grunts. "So what can I do for you, Hank?"

"I'm calling about the investigation you have going on over at Dogtown."

"Oh, aye," Kennedy responded in a thick New England drawl. "Wait, how do you know about that? We've kept it out of the papers so far, and I haven't called in the State for help."

"I know the family," he answered honestly. "It was brought up at the funeral yesterday."

"Son of a bitch," Kennedy replied. "Small world, eh?"

"Small, indeed," Hank echoed. "Too small, maybe."

He paused for a moment and thought through what he needed to say next. If he mentioned that the victim was a childhood friend and that he was interested in getting answers for the family, a man like Richard Kennedy, old friend or not, would shut down and tow the line. If he was to get anything out of this detective, Hank was going to have to tread carefully.

"The family barely knows anything about what happened, and I'm sure you had a lot to do with that. And rightly so."

"Yep, we've tried to keep as many people in the dark about this as possible. Gloucester isn't necessarily the poster child for idyllic city life and crime prevention. Word of a murder in one of our tourist spots, however unsavory the place might be, wouldn't help improve that reputation."

"I agree, and I'm not second guessing your procedure at all, Richard. You're the boss over there. It's your train to drive. But I haven't been around as long as you, and a case like this...well, it's one of those rare things that you can't count on bumping into. I was wondering if you wouldn't mind a couple questions from me. Just to scratch an itch, so to speak."

There was a long pause, and Hank was sure the older officer was searching for the best way to let him down nicely. When Kennedy spoke, though, the reply surprised him.

"Sure, Hank. What are you looking to know?"

Hank exhaled with relief and dove in. "I heard that there was a message written on the boulder near the body. Can you tell me what it said?"

"You know about the Babson boulders, right?" the older man asked. "They've all got something written on them."

"Right," Hank acknowledged. "Something like two-dozen boulders, each with their own carved inscription dating back to the Twenties, right?"

"Yep," Kennedy replied. "This one was the *SAVE* boulder. Probably a message about money. Babson was trying to offer sound financial advice to people suffering through the Depression. Can you believe it? He thought it'd be helpful to tell a bunch of unemployed folk to save their money."

"Irony certainly isn't an invention of the Bush Era," Hank commented and Richard chuckled.

"No, that's for sure. Anyway, the killer added to this message, using the engraving as the first word, you follow?"

"I do," Hank answered. "So what did they add to the stone?"

"This is off the record and very much something you can't go around repeating, even in your office, you understand me, Hank?"

"I do, Richard. I understand very much. This conversation stays between us, end of story."

"Good," Kennedy grunted. "Okay. The killer added four words, written in the victim's own blood.

Together, the message read *SAVE YOURSELF, ALL OF YOU*."

Hank soaked the words in. *All of you*, he thought. *All of* who?

"Do you know what it means?" he asked without any real hope of a helpful answer.

"Not a clue, to be honest. Your thoughts are welcome, though. Let me know if something comes to mind. We're leaving that bit of the investigation behind and chasing after physical evidence, though there's not much of that either."

"What have you recovered from the scene, then?"

Richard paused to cough, and it sounded like a dog was being shot in the office behind him. "Sorry, Barb has me off cigarettes, too. It's doing wonderful things to my voice right now."

Hank chuckled again. "For a woman who stands, what, four-foot-nine and weighs less than the gun I carry, she's certainly got you right where she wants you, old friend."

Richard burst out laughing, which led to more coughing. After a moment, he calmed down and grunted in agreement. "That she does, Hank."

"So, physical evidence?"

"Ah, yes," Kennedy replied, picking up the thread. "We've got very little. Some smudges on the body, but

they're too small to do us any good for now. There's a lot
of disturbance around the boulder itself, like drag marks.
And some odd thick hairs or fibers. That's about it. No
prints, no trails, and certainly no smoking gun laying in
the leaves for us to discover."

"What about the body? Could the victim have
written the message himself?"

Kennedy was quiet for a moment, apparently
thinking. "You know, that's something my people never
considered. His fingers *were* covered in blood. Then again,
so was a lot of him."

Hank winced. "It must be frustrating to not know
more. Thanks for sharing what little you do know with
me, though."

"Always glad to pass along what I know to a
younger pup," Kennedy barked. "I doubt that was enough
to satisfy your curiosity, though. You'd do better watching
old episodes of *CSI*, I think."

Hank laughed. "I'll do that. Thanks Richard. And
enjoy that diet."

"Screw you, Phillips," the older officer replied, but
his voice hinted at the grin he wore. "Take care, and stay
in touch."

"Will do." Hank hung up and sat back in his seat
for a moment. This needed processing. The full message,
the physical evidence, all of it. He patted his left pants

pocket and confirmed that the plastic envelope with its contents was still there. Then, when he felt that he was ready to move on, he buckled his seat belt and shifted the car into drive.

That's when his phone rang again. It was Bill McCarthy.

CHAPTER SEVEN

Bill left Mike's house early on Sunday morning, making the drive from Hollesley to Salem in record time. Apparently, most October tourists didn't consider 6 a.m. on a Sunday to be prime sight-seeing time. The morning air was chill, but nothing compared to what would blow in late December. It was, in fact, unseasonably warm for mid-October.

Once home, Bill parked in the drive and used the front entrance, avoiding the backyard and the broken garage door. He showered and changed before heading down to the kitchen to make himself some breakfast. The back yard was perfectly visible through the window over the sink, but he forced himself to avoid glancing outside.

It was still too early to go next door and tell his neighbors what had happened, so he used the time to get caught up on the mail that had arrived the day before. He had tried to keep his mailing address private, but there were always a few envelopes from fans each week that somehow found their way to him.

He opened one postmarked from Illinois, and read the letter enclosed. It was short and cordial, written out in a beautiful longhand cursive that seemed to be more and more difficult to find these days. The note thanked him for his most recent book, and asked when his next novel might be released.

That's the Million Dollar Question, now, isn't it? he thought. *Well, Rebecca Colehower from Long Point, allow me to introduce you to my editor. You two can have a lovely discussion about my timeline and inability to write fast enough for your liking.*

He tossed the letter onto the growing pile of those that needed responses, and then checked the time. 8:15 a.m. His neighbor, Peter Allaines, would be nearly ready to leave about now. Bill had watched he and his wife back out of their drive nearly every Sunday morning at the exact same time while sitting at his writing desk in the study. He grabbed his phone and stepped out the front door.

The Allaines lived in a similarly large and ancient Federal Style home that exuded charm and classic lines. Their front door was painted glossy black, and Bill mounted the steps and rapped quickly on it. Peter was there, unlocking the door, in less than a minute.

He was a thin man with gray hair, cut short like the beard that covered his jaw. His round glasses reflected the morning light, and the smell of coffee followed him out the door. His shirt, a red and white gingham check, looked sharp beneath the navy sport coat he was wearing.

"Good morning, Bill," he said with a hint of inquisitiveness. "Everything all right?"

Bill smiled sympathetically, and then broke the news. "Hi Peter. No, I'm afraid not." He paused, not sure how to proceed. "I hate to tell you this first thing in the morning, but when I got home last night, I found Vader in my back yard."

"Finally!" Peter sighed. And then, looking over his shoulder, he yelled into the house, "Bill found Vader, honey!"

"No," Bill began, but Sue quickly joined Peter at the door, grinning with gladness. "No, Peter...it's not good news."

The man frowned. "What do you mean, Bill?" he asked, cautiously.

"I came home last night and found an animal in my bushes out back."

He swallowed, glancing at Sue. She wasn't going to take this well, he was certain of that. Ever since their only son, Jacob, was killed in Afghanistan a little over a year ago, she had lived much of her life very near her emotional breaking point. She drifted between overly cheerful—to the point of seeming fake and forced—and a dark melancholy.

Sue Allaines lifted a trembling hand to her face. "Vader?"

Bill gently shook his head. "I'm afraid not, Sue. I found Vader's body in the shrubs behind my oak tree. The animal that did it—I'm assuming a coyote or something similar—also chased me and tried to attack me. I managed to get away and, being the chicken that I am, I ended up spending the night at a friend's house, just to be safe."

Sue seemed to crumple right before his eyes, and Peter turned to support her. He remained stronger than his wife, but it was clear that this news was painful to him as well.

"I..." he began, turning back to Bill. "I'm glad you're all right. Vader...his body...is it...?"

"Yes," Bill answered the unspoken question, saving his neighbor the words. "His body is still back there. To be honest, I've been too nervous to venture out there by myself. But I thought maybe we should let Animal Control take care of the situation. Maybe they can check out the yard and give us an idea of what might have happened."

Peter nodded. "Yes," he said. "I think that's a good idea. No need to take unnecessary risk, of course. Do you think you could have the people from Animal Control remove Vader's body and transport it to our vet? Do they do that?"

"I'm not sure," he shrugged, but smiled warmly. "I'd be happy to ask, and if they need any sort of encouragement," Bill rubbed his thumb across his first two fingertips, "I'll make sure they get what they need."

"Thank you," Peter replied. The man's wife was sobbing quietly in his arms, and her tears were wetting his shirt, giving the red a deeper, more glossy color. Bill noticed how much it looked like blood. "Our vet is Dr. Hammond, just over on Hawthorne Street. Thank you so very much, Bill."

"Hammond, on Hawthorne. Got it. And I'm glad to help. I just wish it were better news, and I'm sorry I couldn't have let you know earlier."

Peter forced a smile while Sue's sobs renewed in earnest. "I understand completely. Thank you again, Bill. Keep us posted if you learn anything more."

Bill nodded, and Peter closed the door gently between them. He glanced once more at the morning sky and the brilliant, colorful trees, and then slipped back into his own home. He had a few phone calls to make.

* * *

Salem Animal Control arrived about an hour later, and Bill stepped out to the driveway to offer the quick tour and details of what had happened. The man who got out of the truck was tall and thick, and his one-piece work suit was unzipped halfway down his chest.

"Damn hot for an Octoba' morning, am I right?" he declared with a thick accent that reminded Bill of the North End of Boston. If the patch on the left side of his chest was to be trusted, the man's name was *Chip*. "Morning," he added, extending a large hand.

Bill shook the hand and introduced himself, wincing at the firmness of the man's grip. "Thanks for coming over so quickly."

Chip shrugged and reached into the back of the truck for a long pole with a loop on the end of it, and then tugged a ratty old Red Sox cap over his receding hairline. The man's age was vague; he could have easily been anywhere between thirty and fifty, and Bill couldn't find a clue that would help him narrow it down.

"Glad to do it," he said, buckling on a utility belt. "When I have a choice, I like to get the house calls out of the way first thing in the morning, before traffic gets too bad. You were closest, so you got first dibs. Where's it at?"

Bill didn't understand the question for the briefest of moments, and then realized the man was asking about Vader's body. He pointed toward the back yard and then led the way. "It's in the bushes behind the big oak, back there. That's where I saw it last, at least. I have no idea if the body was moved by whatever animal killed it."

Chip pulled on a pair of tattered gloves and stepped through the gate. "Let's take a look and see what we can find," he said a little too cheerfully.

Sunlight streamed into the backyard, and the oak that sat sentry at the rear of the property was lit up. The autumn had begun transforming its broad green leaves into gilded scraps that rustled in the breeze. Below the cloud of color ran a long line of dark green shrubs, some evergreen and some holding tightly onto their livelihood. Beyond, there was a small wooden fence and the trees of the property that abutted his.

Bill pointed to the bushes to the left of the large tree. "There," he said cautiously. "I found the dog's body in there."

Chip stepped toward the small bush and pushed the branches aside. "Yep" he said, his voice carrying just enough pleasantness to make Bill's stomach churn. Then, looking back at him, "Christ, where's the head?"

Bill shrugged and nodded at the bushes farther back. "I assumed it was nearby, where ever the animal killed him."

Chip bent low. He grabbed a short stick from the underbrush and began poking around the area where the body lay. He seemed to be studying the corpse, but Bill began to grow uneasy. He could sense Chip's confidence in an easy answer slipping away.

"I'm not so sure about that coyote idea, man," he said without turning back to Bill. "I've seen pets killed by wild animals, but this..." he trailed off. "Damn, the head was ripped off. I've never seen anything like it."

Bill let Chip do his inspection, babbling more about the body, the wound, and the amount of blood in the soil. He even mentioned the quills, but it didn't seem odd to him, at least not as odd as it seemed to Bill himself.

A porcupine couldn't have killed Vader, I know that. He brooded for a moment, wondering what other kind of animal it could have been. *Some kind of wild cat, perhaps? A young bear? Those don't have quills, though.* He wished he had watched more *Wild Kingdom* when he was a boy. He somehow thought that it might have helped him now.

Chip stood up and brushed off his knees. "Ayep," he barked in his thick New England accent. "I think you better call the police."

"The police?" Bill reeled. "For a coyote or wild cat or something like that?"

"Not at all," Chip replied, pulling off his gloves. "That dog was obviously killed by something else. My best guess is it was some sicko, maybe a stalker. Any reason somebody might be crawling around in your back yard?"

Bill shook his head. "No, I can't think of any reasons. I'm not in trouble, no one is pissed at me, and I rarely get fan mail." *Fan mail*, he thought. *Could this be some kind of odd prank by an obsessive fan?*

He had heard of such things happening before. Crime novel writer Patricia Cornwell had trouble with an online stalker, if he recalled. Another, Peter James, who Bill had actually met a few times, had a similar experience. And of course, books like *Misery* didn't instill confidence in a writer's safety if and when a fan went a little nuts. But a mutilated dog? He had his doubts.

"Fan mail?" Chip said with surprise in his voice. "You famous or something?"

"I'm a writer," he replied, hoping that would be enough. "But I've never had crazy fans, before." *Well, that wasn't true*, Bill thought. He wasn't about to tell anyone else about the panties that a fan had mailed to him a few years ago, though. That said, people who mail their underwear to others don't typically go around ripping the heads off of neighborhood dogs.

"Cool," Chip said, and then turned his face back toward the bushes. "Still, I can't take the body now knowing that the police would want to have a look at the scene. Do you want me to give them a call?"

Bill considered the offer, but politely declined. "No, I'll do that myself. Thanks, though."

"All right, then," Chip said. "I'll get out of your hair. But let the police know that if they still want it removed, they can give me a call."

"Will do. Have a good day, and thanks again." Bill nodded his farewell as the man headed back toward the front of the house.

Once inside, he grabbed for his phone. At first, he actually planned to listen to Chip and call the local police. But the thought of a few cops trampling all over his backyard and asking him to explain the night before over and over again seemed far from enticing. He decided he'd rather pass on that mess.

Before he could drop the phone back into his pocket, he had an idea. Maybe Hank could help. He trusted Hank, and it would be a lot better than playing host to a handful of total strangers. Hank knew Bill well enough that he wouldn't jump straight to believing he had lost his mind. And maybe his friend could offer some help without this become something official.

He brought the phone back up and pulled up Hank's number. Then, he took a breath and bushed the button. The phone rang for a moment, and then a familiar voice answered.

"Hey Hank," he said with a sigh with relief. "I need a favor. Can you come over?"

* * *

Hank was sitting in Bill's kitchen within an hour, and both men had a cup of coffee steaming in front of them. Hank's suit coat was hung over the back of his chair, and Bill kept stealing glances at the gun in his friend's exposed shoulder holster.

"Holy crap, man, that's rough," Hank said after Bill finished up with a quick recap of the events of the night before, ending with the advice that Chip from Animal Control had offered. The only pieces he omitted were the quills and the eyes. Those were the details that made him feel as if he were losing his mind, and he wasn't ready to share those bits just yet.

"I'm glad you called. Do you want me to take a look around out there?"

"If you want to," Bill replied. He didn't want to step over any line that might make things awkward between them, but he would certainly welcome Hank's help and trained eyes. "Yeah, that would be great."

The pair stepped outside, and Bill led the way. He walked through the previous night one more time, pointing to the tree and the bushes to anchor the story to real landmarks. Hank listened quietly, nodding and soaking it in.

When they had stepped beneath the oak's branches, Bill pointed out the spot where the body had been, though he didn't come any closer. Hank caught the hint and moved on without him for a better look.

"Can you smell the blood, man?" he asked as he waded into the smaller shrubs. "There was a lot of it. It's like snorting a handful of bad pennies."

"Yeah," Bill replied distantly. He had been breathing through his mouth in an attempt to avoid the odor, but allowed himself a quick sniff. The smell was acrid and sharp and his made his skin crawl.

Hank pushed his large arms through the bushes and parted the thin branches. There was the sound of a twig snapping and then the large man stopped.

"You can see where it had been laying all night. Some of the soil is still dark where the blood pooled. You said the guy from AC couldn't find the head?" He turned and looked back at Bill.

"Nope." Bill motioned to the rest of the yard. "He didn't look everywhere, but I think he worked on the assumption that if an animal had done this, the head would be near enough for us to find."

"That's alright," Hank said, turned back to the place where the body had been found. "Something other than the dog certainly sat in here, though. I can't tell you if it was a coyote or something else, but it was at least as big as the dog."

He bent low, and then straightened back up. The detective turned and cast a glance at Bill that made him think of a child trying—albeit poorly—to hide something that they didn't want someone else to see. He noticed how red Hank's hair appeared when he was wearing a white shirt, and then thought again of the blood.

Hank reached into his back pocket and pulled out a pair of small steel tongs, and then he worked at something in the underbrush. After a moment of quiet work, he slowly rose to his feet and held the tongs in front of his face in the bright sunlight. Finally, he spoke.

"I don't think it was a coyote, Bill." Hank turned and extended the small object in his hand outward. "In fact, I'm positive. And I think this mystery just got a lot bigger than you or I had expected."

"How so?" Bill stepped toward Hank as he spoke, and then stopped, frozen in his tracks, about two feet away. Hank had pinched the metal tool tightly on a small cluster of what looked like long, pale hair.

They were quills.

"Oh, that." He said it as if the word were poisonous. Hank raised an eyebrow.

"*That?* What aren't you telling me, Bill?" His pale skin flushed red and he set his eyes firmly on the other man's. "Talk."

Bill backed up, and then closed his eyes. "I saw them, too. On the body of the dog. Around the neck, where...the place where..."

"These?" Hank held up the tongs again, and the sunlight caught the three long quills that he had managed to pull from the blood-soaked patch of dirt where the dog had been killed and exsanguinated. "I'm not sure what they are, but I have a feeling you do. Or at least, you think you do. Tell me, Bill. What am I looking at here?"

"I don't know!" Bill shouted at his friend. "I don't know...it's a...a memory, I think. Something from our childhood."

"When? The day Kenny died?" Hank's voice was firm but insistent. He wasn't going to let Bill dance around this, that was clear.

"No," he replied, shaking his head. "No, it was from before that. The day we all hiked out at Dogtown. I...I saw something that day."

"Saw what? Dammit, Bill, come on. Spit it out!"

"I don't know! It was behind a tree. We were at the Whale's Jaw, and Kenny was climbing it with George, and I heard something behind me, and for the briefest of moments I thought I saw something move. I didn't really see it, only it's movement. But I remember seeing quills."

Hank's face was frozen in shock. "At Dogtown? You saw something with quills out at Dogtown?"

Bill took another step back. He could feel Hank's anger, but he wasn't sure it was directed at him. "Yes, but why is that important? It was over twenty years ago. This," he pointed hard at the bushes, "was last night, in my *back yard*, Hank. *Here*."

Hank took a breath and closed his eyes for a moment. Once he had calmed, he reached into his pocket with a free hand and pulled out an opaque plastic envelope. He extended it to Bill.

"Look inside, but don't touch what's inside."

Bill took the envelope with a shaking hand but didn't take his eyes off of Hank's. It was clear that his friend was trying to make a point, and it frightened him. Finally, he broke eye contact and looked at what Hank had given him.

The envelope reminded him of the experience of buying stamps at the post office as a kid. His parents had suggested that it would be good for him to have a hobby, and he finally settled on stamps. While he had limited access to old postage stamps, he was free to purchase new collector sets as they were released. And every set he bought came in a flat, waxy envelope similar to this one.

Folding back the flap, he glanced inside and then closed his eyes with a sigh. More quills.

"Where are these from?" He handed the envelope back to Hank with a shaking hand. "No, I think I already know. Dogtown, right?"

Hank nodded. "I was there this morning. I was leaving when you called me."

"Doing what?"

"Taking a look for myself. George deserves it," he said. Then, after a pause, "Deserved, I guess. I wanted answers."

"And did you find any?" Bill stood up a little straighter and forced himself to calm down. He took a deep breath and could smell the slight rotting scent of autumn leaves and mulch mingled with blood.

"A few," Hank replied. "But I think I still have more questions than answers. And after this," he motioned to the bushes with the envelope, "I'm not sure where to go from here."

"Well, maybe we should look at this like a novel." Bill flashed a shy smile. "The characters in detective stories always run through the list of things they are certain of, and then jump off from that point. So, what do we know?"

"We know," began Hank, "that George was killed in Dogtown by someone who left no clues behind other than these things." He waved the envelope one last time, and then pushed it back into his pocket. "We know that you were attacked by what you *think* was a wild animal, and that whatever it was also left behind quills."

"We also know that porcupines aren't vicious killers," Bill added, and Hank grunted a short laugh.

"So, the only mystery now is what the connection is between your backyard and Dogtown. And that just doesn't seem logical. Other than your friendship to him, you had very little else in common with George."

Bill thought for a moment. "He did enjoy my books. At least, that's what he told me. In fact, I think he was the only one of you guys who told me so."

Hank shook his head. "No, I doubt it could be that. Unless you have some sort of an angry fan stalking you and anyone else who enjoys your books. But I think the odds of them knowing about George seem pretty slim."

"So, I guess we don't know much, do we?" Bill's shoulders slumped.

"Not yet. But I'll keep looking into it, and we both need to keep our ears open for anything that might connect the dots."

Bill nodded. "And keep an eye out for rabid porcupines in the mean time, right?"

"Exactly." Hank smiled, and the two men walked back to the house, the warm and sunny morning air ignorant of their dark mood.

CHAPTER EIGHT

Mike had pulled into the lot at Midtown Café a few moments before, but had yet to walk inside. His hands were still to the steering wheel and his vision had narrowed to a small tunnel focused solely on the front door of the restaurant. He was waiting for the men he had seen to leave.

They had entered just as Mike was pulling in. He had glanced down to find his phone and when he sat back up they were there. One of them was a complete stranger, but the other man was a potential trigger for Mike's guilt: Daniel Tobey.

Mike sat in his car for a few minutes, talking himself into going inside the café. He knew that he couldn't keep avoiding the man, but it was more than a little awkward nonetheless. Daniel's presence had a way of making him feel guilty, certainly, but Mike knew he would eventually need to decide that he wasn't going to let he guilt rule him any longer.

Of course, Daniel had never done anything to intentionally cause him to feel guilty. Mike was fully aware that his feelings were self-generated. Kenny's father had not said something blaming or accusatory toward him, neither immediately after the accident nor in the subsequent twenty years that had followed. Logically, Mike had no reason to feel this way.

What Mike wanted, more than anything else in the entire world, was to be able to release this guilt. To set it free and watch it float away like a balloon. But in moments like these, he couldn't help but feel that freedom would never be entirely possible.

He was going to have to make changes to move toward that healing. He understood that. Yet he sat frozen in his car rather than doing what he had come to do—buy an iced coffee—and that made him feel foolish. He *was* a fool, but perhaps today was the day for that to stop.

As if an internal football coach had shouted at him and then slapped his ass, Mike's eyes shot open wide. He forced the guilt into a corner of his gut and then opened the car door. Once he swung his left foot over to the pavement, it was like a spell had been broken. He could do this. He was sure of it.

Progress, he thought. *I've got to start somewhere, right?*

He entered the restaurant quickly, made a bee-line for the counter, and quickly ordered his drink.

"That'll be $3.43," the girl behind the counter said. She couldn't have been more than seventeen, but she had the bored and disinterested expression of someone who had been performing their job for far too long.

Mike handed over four bills and when she handed back his change, he tossed it into the mug beside the register. The mug was bright red, and had white text on it that instructed everyone to *Keep Calm and Drink Coffee*. Mike smiled and then turned to face the restaurant and find a seat while he waited for his drink to be made.

He immediately made eye contact with Daniel Tobey.

"Mike," Daniel said. He waved a hand to catch his attention. "Good to see you."

Mike did his best to smile, though he was sure it looked more like a grimace, and approached the table where the two men sat. Daniel pulled a chair out for him and then extended a hand.

"Good to see you again," Daniel said warmly.

Mike thought that the man looked tired, but it could also be the effects of the same emotional roller-coaster that he and the others had been on the last few days.

The man wore a brown jacket with white dust in the creases and frayed edges on the cuffs. His features were strong and sharp, but Mike noticed the age in his face now. Daniel seemed to have diminished slightly in the day since the funeral.

Mike shook his hand and took a seat reluctantly. "Likewise." And then, turning to the man beside Daniel, he extended his hand and introduced himself. "Mike Barton."

The man, who appeared to be in his late fifties, shook Mike's hand and smiled. "Joe Ravenwood. Pleased to meet you."

Mike recognized the name, and now the face made sense. Joe, he had heard around town, was fully Native American, a direct descendent from the Indians who had lived in the New England area since long before Europeans had arrived. In fact, among the Wampanoag people that still remained, Joe was considered a respected elder.

In Hollesley, though, he was owner of Ravenwood Realty, the largest independent real estate company on the North Shore. Mike had heard the name for years, but his professional circle never seemed to overlap with Joe's.

The older man's face was chiseled and dark, and his black hair was straight and long, pulled back behind his neck. His gray suit was as professional as could be expected, but Mike noticed a small pin on his lapel, a pink ring with a maroon star in the center.

"Likewise," Mike replied. "I've heard a lot about you. All good things, I promise." He smiled and the others laughed.

"Daniel and I were just talking about work. He keeps my rental properties in tip-top shape, and handles any remodeling that might need done. What about you, Mike? What do you do for work?"

"I manage a team of number crunchers at a local accounting firm," Mike replied.

"You're an accountant, then?"

Mike nodded. "Yes. Well, I do more management at this point, so I see a few less spreadsheets than I used to. It sounds like an improvement to most people, but I miss it sometimes. Numbers are my comfort zone."

"I can understand that," Joe said. "I got into this business over thirty years ago because I loved sales. Nothing beats walking a new homeowner through a house and helping them see the potential. Now," he sighed and glanced at his hands, "well, I haven't done a showing in years."

"Yeah, but you captain the whole ship," added Daniel. "That has its own perks."

"Sure, but it's just not the same. You still get to work on-site each day, doing what you enjoy." He turned back to Mike. "You understand what I mean, don't you? No amount of managerial power can replace the thrill of doing what you love."

"Absolutely." Mike had missed the daily grind ever since his office moved and he was put in charge of his first group of coworkers. Management was more centered on people; numbers were where he felt safe. Numbers were predictable and errors were concrete and easy to repair when you found them. People were 'a bag of hurt', to borrow a phrase he had heard once. They came with complications.

A young woman approached the table, carrying Mike's iced coffee. She smiled as she set it down, and then quickly vanished back into the chaos behind the counter.

"Iced coffee, eh?" Daniel said. "In October?"

"Sure thing. It's been nearly as warm as June these past couple of weeks. I can't remember the last time we had an Indian summer this powerful." Mike stopped the moment the words had left his mouth, worried he had offended Joe. He glanced at him with wide eyes.

Joe picked up on the expression and chuckled. "Don't worry about it. There are plenty of things that offend my people, but that's not one of them."

Mike sighed. "Thanks."

Daniel leaned forward. "Some say it's called Indian Summer because it meant that the Indians were returning for more blood."

"Is that so?" Mike asked politely.

"When the white men first settled here, they had to be armed all through the summer months because the Indians constantly attacked them. When the cooler weather came, the Indians would stop and the settlers would be able to leave their forts unarmed. The unexpected return of warm weather meant the return of the Indians with it."

"I was raised to understand that it was actually a blessing." Joe motioned toward the windows. "Sometimes the harvest was difficult to bring in on time. Heat waves like this offered Native Americans a chance to finish the harvest before winter shut things down for good."

"Seize the day," Mike added.

"Absolutely," said Joe. "Speaking of which, while most people refuse to work on Sundays, I need to get back to my office. The empire won't run itself, unfortunately."

The three of them stood, and Mike extended a hand once more. "It was a pleasure to meet you, Joe."

"Likewise, Mike," Joe replied.

"Good to see you, Mike. I'm sure I'll see you around town sooner or later," he extended a hand and smiled at him.

Mike shook the hand again, and noticed this time he felt much less anxiety. *Maybe there's hope*, he thought. Picking up his drink, he headed toward the door. The unusually warm October air brushed against his skin as he walked outside and, for the first time in a very long time, Mike felt free.

* * *

Steve Bowers stood in the hallway outside his daughters' room that evening, staring at the open door. He could only see a slim black vertical line in the dim light of the hall but it was enough to tell him the door was ajar. That troubled him; he was positive that he had closed it just three hours before.

It had been a hectic evening, that was sure. Beth was out, spending the evening over at the food bank in order to help them get caught up. Margaret Ashcroft, George's mother, was the cornerstone of the shop and without her things had quickly fallen into chaos. Beth had hoped that an extra set of hands might help out.

It had been another successful evening of putting the girls to bed, though. Well, success in the sense that bedtime lacked any of the usual fighting, crying or jumping on the bed. This marked two nights in a row, quite an accomplishment considering all of the variables and opportunity for random meltdowns.

He had come downstairs right after leaving their room, and he was sure he had pulled their door closed behind him. There was a lot on his mind, though, so he was willing to accept that he might have forgotten. But Steve was very fond of his routines, and he was certain that, even unconsciously, he would have repeated that final nightly chore.

The girls' room was at the top of the stairs, and he had a deep fear that if the door were left open all night, one of the kids might walk out to use the bathroom and fall down the steps. That fear drove his routine, and the idea that he might have forgotten to shut the door tonight left him feeling unnerved.

He shook his head and pulled the door closed. *Again*, he thought. *I'm closing it again.* He didn't make mistakes like this. He wouldn't be able to live with himself if something bad happened. He reminded himself to check it one last time before heading to bed, and to also check the knob hardware in the morning. It was an old house, and there was the chance—however slim—that the door just didn't catch the first time.

Steve walked down the hall to the bedroom he shared with Beth and turned on the small lamp on the nightstand closest to the door. He swapped out his button-up shirt for a t-shirt and sweatshirt in an effort to get more comfortable, and after putting on his slippers, he headed back downstairs to take care of some of his email ahead of Monday morning.

He had worked at Terraprint, a local print company, for nearly a decade now. Though he had studied design in college, he found the freelance world much too competitive and managed to use some connections to move into a sales job assisting customers with print orders.

The job had a lot of variety built into it, and while some Monday mornings might be spent catching up on all of his weekend email, he was often pulled to the print floor without warning to check a proof or make a selection between two paper stock options.

Steve liked to get ahead of the game and knock out as much of his email as possible on Sunday nights. Tonight that task was quick, and he found himself with a bit more free time than usual. If there was something that parenthood lacked, it was free time, and he was never one to pass up a good thing.

He walked to the kitchen and pulled a wine glass from the cupboard beside the sink. A small glass of port sounded like a fine reward after an evening with the girls. But as he turned to walk toward his stash of liquor, he saw a flash of light through the window.

Actually, there was more than one light. There were dozens of small points of light, floating slowly through the air. They reminded him of the fireflies that made their appearance during the summer, but these were more pale and cold and they moved much slower. None of them winked, though, and that made it all the more eerie to watch. It was as if there were dozens of people standing in the dark outside his home, wandering back and forth with small, blue-white lanterns.

He set the glass back down and leaned closer to the window. They were almost hypnotic, moving gently back and forth. Their light was soothing, and Steve felt a deep longing to be closer. Without thinking, he turned and moved toward the back door and out into the yard.

The air outside was cool but pleasant. He could feel his slippers growing damp and cold and he walked across the lawn. That didn't stop him from moving forward toward the lights, though. Or were they pulling him? He couldn't be sure. All he knew was that he needed to be closer.

He faintly remembered Sarah saying something about *sparkling tights*. No, it was *lights*. She said there were lights—pretty lights—that floated. In the backyard, in fact.

Walking through the darkness toward the edge of the yard, Steve began to understand. They were indeed pretty, and his feet kept moving toward them, step by step, as if a rope had been tied around his waist and he were being led.

One drifted close and he reached out a trembling hand to touch it. The light remained within reach until his fingers were nearly upon it, and then slowly drifted away, blown by a wind Steve could not feel. He stepped closer, again trying to touch one of the ethereal lights. Each attempt had the same frustrating result.

He could feel water around his slippers now, and understood on a subconscious level that he had exited his yard and was moving into the wetlands beyond. It didn't matter, though. Nothing mattered at that moment, save the near-hypnotic attraction of the lights.

Steve felt water around his ankles now. Another light came close and he reached higher, nearly wrapping his fingers around its cold blue lights. At the last moment the light drifted lazily through his fingers, and he stumbled forward, almost losing his balance.

He was about to move forward again, drawn by the lights, when the backyard lit up in a yellow glow, and he blinked as if waking from a dream. From somewhere behind him he could hear the sound of Beth's minivan pulling down the gravel drive. In an instant, the spell was broken and he turned to look.

Her headlights had illuminated the back yard, and Steve was surprised to see that he was standing a dozen or more paces into the wetlands with cold, muddy water collecting around his knees. He panicked, not sure of how he had gotten there, and then remembered the lights. When he glanced back, however, all he could see now was darkness over the wet earth.

The lights, whatever they had been, were gone. Carefully, moving one foot at a time, Steve made his way back toward the house. He knew he would have to explain to his wife why his slippers and pants were soaked with brown water, but his mind struggled to find an explanation. Just the lingering feeling of discovery and loss, of having reached the threshold of something powerful, only to have had the door closed on him too soon.

CHAPTER NINE

While Steve Bowers was wringing out his slippers in an effort to get dry, Roger O'Connor was about as wet as he could get. The large plastic cup from the Sunoco down the street, a prized possession because of a misprint on the side that advertised *fill service* rather than *full service*, had just been filled with half of the contents of a plastic bottle of vodka.

Roger didn't make it a habit to get drunk the night before an early shift at work, but he was making an exception this evening. Most of life was tolerable for him; he had a steady job that allowed him to work by himself most of the time, and he had a few friends to call when he had time off. But George's funeral the day before had really set him off balance.

And then Sheila had called.

Sheila, who most of his friends would know primarily by the moniker *The Bitch*, was Roger's ex-wife. They had parted ways—about as far from amicably as two people could, mind you—nearly a decade ago. There had been no kids to fight over, or even a house to split up.

It was the classic, nearly stereotypical breakup where Roger's belongings ended up flying out the window of the fourth story and landing in a broken heap on the apartment building's front lawn.

It was far from Roger's fault. She had cheated on him, and when he found out, he had confronted her. The fault, it seems, rested on Roger's complete lack of tact. The method he chose to let her know he had discovered the affair was to scribble a hateful message on the bathroom mirror with her lipstick, and then drink himself stupid until she had returned from a late night working the bar at *Smitty's*.

Roger lacked delicacy, but he was also want for a backbone. As a result, instead of kicking Sheila out on her cheating ass, she had tossed *him* out. It helped that she was sober and he wasn't. It also helped that the boyfriend she threatened to call was a full foot taller than he was and had arms as big around as a telephone pole.

Throwing his things out the window was the first hint. The phone call to her lover was the second. That was all it took, too. Fifteen minutes after she had come home from work—including the three minutes she spent yelling at him for getting wasted on a work night before she had even walked into the bathroom—he was crawling around in the wet grass, collecting his clothing and broken LP's in his scrawny arms.

The divorce could have been seen as freedom.
Many would have used the chance to make a fresh start.
But Sheila was the type of woman to keep as many
options open as possible. She kept a lot of things open,
apparently, but it would have been dangerous to point
things like that out to her. Whenever she found herself
without a boyfriend, or just needed a body to warm her
bed, she called Roger.

Roger found it easier to reject her offers in the first
few months after the divorce. His emotions were still raw
and the hatred had yet to stop running hot and deep.
After a few breakups of his own, though, her temptations
managed to take a foothold in his heart, like kudzu
creeping up a stone wall. She was just as destructive, too.

He had spent the last eight years serving her
whims and needs, strung along by whatever slender thread
of affection had managed to escape the shearing during
the divorce. When she needed him, she called, and Roger
rarely said no. While this surely kept him busy, it had the
nasty side-effect of preventing him from building another
relationship to replace her.

This was by design, and Roger slowly caught on to
that. He had been dodging her calls lately and pretending
to not be home when she came knocking on his door. She
said sweet things and she said mean things, but she kept
turning up regardless, like a bad penny. Roger knew that if

he was to have any hope of building something better in his future, he needed to cut her off for good.

Now he stood in the living room of his small, filthy apartment holding a plastic jumbo-sized cup full of cheap vodka, staring out the window that looked out on the street and wharf area beyond. He had left the lights off, feeling more comfortable in the darkness. It worked a lot like the alcohol; while the drink numbed his mind, the darkness dulled his other senses. And Roger was in the mood to feel as little as possible.

George's death had hit him harder than he was willing to admit to the others. All of them probably felt that way to a degree, but Roger was certain he was the most devastated by it. Granted, Mike was having a hard time dealing with it, but Mike had a hard time dealing with anything that wasn't a promotion or an attaboy on the backside. No, Mike's grief was more systemic.

Roger, though, had spent much of the last two decades on fantastic terms with nearly everyone in their old group of friends, Mike being the exception. He and Bill had managed to remain tight through the years, despite his friend's increase in fame and personal wealth. Bill was good people, something he always said when people found out he was friends with a famous author.

If anyone avoided him at all it might be Hank, but Roger assumed that was because Hank spent his days

chasing people who made poor life decisions, and a
divorced alcoholic house painter didn't make for the best
professional association. When they were together, Hank
was just as warm and friendly as he had always been, so
maybe it was really just Hank's all-consuming job that
kept him distant.

Steve was normal and pleasant, and Roger
managed to get him out for drinks every couple of
months. Steve was probably the closest thing to a blue-
collar guy that the group had beside himself, and that
helped their bond. He was devoted to his family, which
wasn't a bad thing, but it did make him less available for
get-togethers.

Which led back to Sheila. Sheila, who had robbed
him of a chance at happiness. Sheila, who had been using
him for years, as one might use a pair of hedge clippers—
occasionally and as needed. And now, at the end of an
emotionally exhausting weekend following the death of a
childhood friend, it was Sheila who had volunteered to
kick him while he was down.

He had woken up late in the morning after
spending the previous evening drowning his depression
with as much liquid medication as possible. Starting the
day with the hangover to end all hangovers was not
Roger's preference, but the bright side was that the

constant throbbing in his left temple helped keep his mind off of George.

After a lunch small enough to not risk more nausea, he had shuffled down the street to his favorite packy, a hole in the wall called *Hamilton's*, where he purchased four of the 1.5-liter jugs of his favorite vodka. Then he had slowly, painfully returned home.

When he got there, the phone was ringing. The sound was like a high-powered drill pressed up against the side of head, and it took all of his concentration to unlock the door in time to answer it. The voice on the other end was even more of an assault on his senses, though, and when they were done talking, his head felt like it had been halved by a log splitter.

It had been Sheila, of course. She was the master of the out of the blue moment. Roger couldn't remember if she had ever told him ahead of time that she would be calling or visiting. That would have been too kind, too helpful, both of which were characteristics that Sheila lacked.

But her phone call today had not been the typical cry for attention that he was used to hearing. She had called to tell him that her boyfriend had proposed and that she was getting married and that she could finally stop looking. It was the kind of passive-aggressive conversation that she was a master of starting; on the surface she had innocently called to share her good news, but that news was also designed to drive a spike through Roger's heart.

That had been hours ago. Since then he had polished off the first of the large bottles he had purchased after lunch, and was deep into the second. He wanted to be numb, to no longer feel, and to find some silver lining in Sheila's phone call. But if he was completely honest with himself, he had never really moved on from her. There had never been a need; she was always there when she had the time or desire, and that had been enough for him.

Roger pulled his only recliner over to the large picture window, pointed it out toward the dark glass and the city lights beyond, and sunk into it. It was a low, wide armchair that he had found on the side of the road years before, and though the floral patterns of yellow and blue were far from his personal choice, it worked and was comfortable.

From this seat he could see the slowly moving yellow lights of the few boats still active in the wharf, each one breaking up the darkness like dim, moving stars. Their slow, sideways drift from one edge of the windowpane to the other was hypnotic, and Roger barely registered his oncoming drowsiness before he was asleep.

He didn't know how long he had slept, but it was still dark when he opened his eyes. There were fewer boats in the wharf, that was certain, but having no watch on his wrist or clock on the wall made it impossible to say for sure. The room was still pitch black, save for the pale yellow glow that spilled in through the window. Something seemed different, though.

He could hear breathing.

For a moment, Roger was sure that Sheila had returned. She had obviously seen the error of her decision, recognized just how much she needed him, and had come in the middle of the night to tell him. Then he noticed how quickly, how somehow small and miniature, the breathing sounded. It wasn't the breathing of an adult; it had the sound of someone or something smaller, perhaps the size of a child.

Roger turned to look over his shoulder, but something strange happened. His brain fired the message, and his eyes turned in their sockets to meet the view, but his body refused to budge.

He tried again, but the result was the same. He couldn't turn his head. He reached up to feel his neck, and then realized that his arm hadn't moved either. *There it is*, he thought, *just sitting on my leg. What the hell?*

He had slept in some odd positions throughout his life, and had awoken on many occasions with an arm or leg completely asleep. This was far from a numb limb, though. He couldn't move his body.

He kicked his feet outward, leaned forward and flipped his head backwards, but nothing happened. The sensation was there, but nothing was moving. He was paralyzed, frozen in place and unable to move his body. And he could still hear the breathing.

He rolled his eyes to their limits, scanning what little of the room he could see with his peripheral vision. There was nothing to be seen to his immediate left or right, but something else caught his attention. Something on his chest.

It was a dart, or at least, it looked like one. There was a small, thin object protruding from his chest, a few inches below his clavicle. It looked like a very thin piece of wood, but it was rough and uneven, like a twig. Whatever it was, it had been whittled to a needle-sharp point. Something green and wispy—hair perhaps, or moss?— had been wound around the end like some attempt at fletching.

Roger tried to swear, but his mouth failed to cooperate. The only sound he made was a low, guttural moan. He couldn't move, couldn't speak, and couldn't see whomever it was that waited behind him. The only thing that still seemed to function normally at the moment was his breathing, though even that had become shallow and labored.

Movement caught his eye somewhere off to his right, and he strained to study the peripheral of his vision. The shape that stepped into the light, a dim and yellow glow cast by a street lamp somewhere outside the window, turned his blood cold.

The first things he saw were the eyes. They were bright red and set wide in a gray face. The nose and ears were large and exaggerated, and thin hair grew in patches around the chin and the top of the head.

The creature itself was about the height a child, but stocky and wide. It wore a torn piece of brown cloth around its body like a cloak. Its shoulders were hunched, and protruding from its back through the fabric were hundreds of sharp quills. It was as if a porcupine were hidden beneath the cloth.

Roger thought it resembled what his childhood mind would have dreamed up as a troll. Whatever the misshapen and malformed creature was—troll or goblin or whatever it was—it now stood only a few feet away from him, just on the edge of the shadows. And Roger could hear it breathing.

It didn't speak. Roger wasn't even sure if it could, but he was sure his current muteness somehow clouded his judgment. Something about the creature seemed very feral and savage, though, and fear was welling up inside him like bile. He struggled yet again to move, but his body refused to obey.

Its wide, snout-like nose twitched like a dog sniffing the air outside, and then a grin split the flesh of its face. Behind those thin, drawn lips was a set of teeth that looked as sharp as knives and as small as needles. It was the creature's eyes, though, that drove the spike of fear completely through his heart. They were red and piercing and seemed to draw his gaze. He couldn't look away.

When it stepped closer, Roger's mind practically exploded with panic. He tried to rock himself out of the chair, but his body remained glued to the seat. He was trapped and powerless, even though there wasn't a single bond on him. No rope, no chains, no wires or bindings. He was free to run, yet completely incapable of doing so.

His mind screamed. It roared and wailed and filled his thoughts with blinding fear. His heart was pounding so fast that he expected it to explode in his chest. His stomach felt like it was full of a cocktail of bile and cement and rusty nails. Then the creature was close enough for him to smell it.

It wasn't an unpleasant scent. Roger would have said it was almost floral. The creature seemed crafted of pure nature and smelled as if it had rolled in green grass and dead leaves before coming here. It wasn't the putrid, nauseating odor of decay that one might expect from a fairy tale monster.

One small, gnarled hand reached out toward him, and he felt his body try to recoil and fail. The flesh of the hand was a pale gray color, and the fingernails looked more like claws than anything human. With painful slowness, the hand was creeping closer.

And then it stopped.

It was inches away, and out of the corner of his eye Roger could see every wrinkle and crack on the outstretched fingers. Then the hand moved to touch the arm of the recliner he was siting in. There was a moment where great tension was visible in the fingers, as if they were straining against a heavy weight, and then there was fire.

Flames, small and hungry, licked out from the tips of its fingers and caressed the old fabric of the armchair. One of the yellow flowers slowly changed color to tan, then brown, and then, just as it became black, the flame caught and blossomed. Roger could smell melted plastic and charred wood, and his eyes opened wide with horror.

He didn't see the creature leave. Within seconds, the smoke from the burning chair had blocked his view to either side. What little air he had been managing to inhale was quickly becoming too toxic and smoky. He couldn't cough. He couldn't move. The chair was on fire and his body refused to run to safety.

Roger could see the lights in the wharf moving slowly from right to left and left to right. He could hear the crackling of the blazing fabric beneath and behind him. The sensation of heat was spreading and intensifying, and his back and arms felt like they were blistering. Along with the pain and panic, he was starting to feel faint. Very little oxygen was making it through the smoke that now billowed up from beneath him.

Black spots swam before his eyes and the floor began to feel like it was moving. His head ached and the sound of the growing fire was all he could hear. Heat buffeted the back of his neck like a hateful kiss.

The last thing Roger saw before he lost consciousness was the lights from the boats, each one moving about as if nothing was wrong. Moments after losing consciousness, his clothing and hair ignited in a mantle of orange and yellow light. Long before his brain could begin to cry out for oxygen, his skin had begun to redden, then blister, and finally blacken.

Had anyone glanced up from the street at the large picture window above *Eddie's Beef and Seafood*, they would have seen a brilliant orange glow, and perhaps even the dark silhouette of an arm chair at the center of the flames. Roger, though, was gone, his body charred and reduced to nothing more than a smoldering husk.

CHAPTER TEN

Hank's Monday morning began much earlier that he had expected, and when he arrived at the crime scene on Derby Street, he knew the day was only going to get worse.

The sun had barely begun to cast a pale yellow glow across the eastern sky when he took the exit off Route 128 toward Salem. There was a wisp of fog in the ditches along the highway as the unusual heat of the morning air vaporized the dew. And though it was mid-October, traffic heading into Salem had yet to become as frustratingly slow as it would be in another hour.

When he arrived, there were four city police cruisers parked near the corner of Derby and Turner, as well as a Salem Fire and Rescue ladder truck and the coroner's car. Hank slipped under the yellow tape that marked off the area in front of *Eddie's Beef and Seafood* and approached the officer who was standing watch at the door to the apartments above.

"No entry, sir." The officer was much younger than Hank, possibly in his first year on the job, and he barely made eye contact before returning his gaze to the traffic in the street.

"Detective Phillips," Hank responded. He flashed his identification at the man. "Massachusetts State Police."

The officer's head snapped back around. Recognition and surprise washed over his face before he quickly moved out of the way.

"Go right up, sir,' he stammered. "Detective Mansfield is in charge of the scene, and he's upstairs already. Sorry, sir."

"Thanks."

Hank stepped into the doorway and instinctively ducked. He was a tall man, and he had knocked his head against the low-hanging HVAC ductwork that crossed the hallway on more than one occasion. He sighed, knowing it was probably the last time he would enter Roger's apartment.

He ascended the stairs swiftly, taking two at a time until he reached the landing at the top. A short hallway branched off to the right, leading to two filthy doors, one on either side. The door on the right was wide open, and more yellow tape was hung across the opening.

He bent low and passed beneath the tape. One officer stood in the kitchen, and beside him was a second dressed in street clothes. He was on the phone, and his free hand was scribbling notes on a pad of paper he had set on the counter. Hank nodded at the first officer and flashed his badge before stepping into the room.

The stench of charred fabric, wood, and flesh immediately assaulted him. The room was dark, but didn't seem to be any filthier than Roger had usually kept it. The only area that seemed different was the living room, straight ahead from the apartment door.

Hank walked through the small kitchen and stepped into the space where Roger had kept a small tube television and a coffee table covered in car magazines and catalogues. The table had been a roadside find, and he remembered helping his friend haul it up the stairs after he had found it. In fact, that had been the very first time he had bashed his head against the HVAC duct in the entryway.

Beyond the table the room felt unfamiliar. It looked as if his friend had pulled the beat-up recliner over to face out the front window. Little of the chair remained, however. A blackened skeleton of charred wood and shreds of fabric sat in the center of a dark, damp circle on the floor.

The air was filled with an acrid scent, and Hank brought a hand up to cover his nose as he stepped closer. There was little left of the chair, but he could see thin, broken lines among the carnage that he knew instinctively were bones. It was Roger.

Hank fought his emotions for a moment and turned his head away toward the broken glass of the picture window to clear his mind. He stepped closer to it and took a few deep breaths. There would be time to mourn his friend—yet another friend—after his work was done. Now was not the time to be weak.

He returned his gaze to the room and saw that the officer in plain clothes was off the phone and heading his way. Hank moved toward him in order to put the skeletal remains of the chair behind him.

"Detective Phillips?" The man extended a hand to Hank. He looked to be about middle-aged, and his face had the seasoned look of a cop who had seen far too much in his career for his own good. His hair was cropped short, but Hank could see the gray that was slowly taking over the area near his temples.

"That's me," he replied, shaking the man's hand. "Thanks for letting me visit your scene."

"No problem," the man replied. "Detective Mansfield. Feel free to call me Jim, though."

"Hank works for me, too."

"How'd you hear about our little incident here?" Mansfield asked politely. "I don't need help, and don't remember telling anyone to call in the MSP. Don't get me wrong, you're not unwelcome, I'm just not sure what you can offer besides an extra pair of eyes."

"That's all I wanted to offer, so we're on the same page." Hank looked around. "To be honest, I have a personal connection. The victim, Roger O'Connor, was a childhood friend. When I heard what had happened, I wanted to have a look for myself. I hope that's all right with you. You're in charge, and I'll defer to your decision, of course."

Mansfield sighed. "Sorry to hear. I've had the displeasure of investigating the deaths of two separate friends over the years, so I completely understand that blurry line between our job and our lives. Look around. Any insight you have would be helpful. There's not much evidence here, and for the moment we're leaning toward accidental death as a result of smoking in a chair doused in alcohol."

Hank shook his head. "I don't buy that. Roger wasn't a smoker. Odd, of course, for a guy who drank so much, but he never touched a cigarette in his life."

"Well, judging by the amount of booze we found in the kitchen, and the empties in the trash, your buddy had enough fuel in him to launch a rocket. If it wasn't cigarettes, then there must be an ignition source somewhere. I'll have my forensics team look deeper and try to find an answer."

"Sounds good," Hank said. "I'll take a look around and let you know if I see anything odd."

"Perfect," said Mansfield. "And I'm sorry for your loss, Detective Phillips. Losing a friend hurts."

Hank forced a smile. "Thanks, Jim."

He knew what he was looking for. After learning of George's murder—Hank was unwilling to think of it as anything but that—and the attack on Bill, he was almost positive he would find quills here as well. It was a matter of searching, and hoping that the fire didn't destroy the evidence.

He knew he would find what he was looking for, but that didn't mean he wanted to. The quills didn't answer any of their questions. All they did was tie together the violence that had fallen upon his small group of childhood friends. They failed to tell him who was behind the attacks, or the reason for them. Those were questions that he was going to have to work out for himself.

He turned back to the husk of the armchair and began to walk slowly around it, looking at the chair and the carpet it sat on. Judging by the shards of glass that littered the area in front of the chair, the first responders had approached the fire from outside. He could understand how that would have been easier than coming up the narrow stairs to the third floor, but it certainly made a mess of the crime scene.

Hank's feet crunched as he took slow, deliberate paces around what remained of Roger and the recliner. It made searching the floor for anything out of the ordinary extremely challenging, but knowing what he was looking for helped him focus.

The urge to weep rose up once more, but he beat it down like some morbid game of Whack-a-Mole. *Not now,* he thought. *There's time for that when this is figured out. Work it, Hank. Work the clues and chase the truth. You can manage this.*

He had travelled around so that the chair was to his right and he was facing the window. Looking out the opening in the apartment wall, he could see the peaks of the House of Seven Gables and the wharf beyond them. Boats moved slowly across the field of blue and disappeared behind buildings, and then reappeared again.

Looking down, he continued to scan the carpet again. It was old and shaggy, and the mauve color had been bleached by the sunlight from the window into a muted pink. The broken glass lay scattered across it like diamonds, twinkling up at him. All he could smell, though, was the charred fabric and wood of the chair.

He pulled a pen out of his suit pocket and poked at the glass here and there. Where two pieces would overlap, their edges would create a pale, thin line that looked very similar to the quills he was hoping to find. He moved slowly and kept flipping over the pieces.

Then he saw one. Just one quill, nothing more. But it was the same long, narrow hair-like fiber that he had seen before. It was just a couple of feet from the base of the chair, but he was certain that it had no earthly reason for being there in the first place.

He glanced over his shoulder and noticed that Mansfield was just a few paces away, looking in his direction. Picking up the quill now, in front of the man, would probably look suspicious, and leaving the crime scene with it wouldn't be possible at all. The last thing he needed was to get in trouble for overstepping his boundaries.

Hank decided that it would be better to just leave the quill where it was. He knew what they looked like, and he had found the connection he was looking for. This particular quill had already served its purpose.

He shrugged and stood, turning to face Mansfield. "Nothing. This place is barren. I don't envy your investigation."

Mansfield forced a smile and nodded. "It's what we do, right? Gather the evidence and then follow the trail if we can. Sometimes it just doesn't work out."

Well," Hank said. "I hope it does this time. Roger was a good friend, and having some closure would be helpful, but I know how hard your job can be. Best of luck, Jim."

The men shook hands. "Thanks, Hank. I'll give you a call if I learn anything new. And I'm sorry about your loss, honestly."

"I appreciate that. Thanks."

With that, he crossed the apartment and slipped out the door. Hank waited until he had descended the stairs and stepped out onto the sidewalk before pulling the phone out of his pocket. He tapped it a few times and then held it to his ear before walking toward his car.

"Hello?" Bill's voice answered nervously from the other end of the line.

"Hey, it's Hank." He paused for a moment, looking for the right words. "Bill, there was a fire at Roger's place late last night. Roger...he...oh man, this is tough...Bill, he's dead."

There was only silence for a moment.

"You've already been to his place, haven't you? Were you looking for what I think you were?"

"Yeah," he said without emotion.

"And you found more quills, didn't you?"

"Yeah." He had reached his car and climbed in, shutting the door between himself and the warm morning air.

"God, not Roger too. Dammit, what's happening, Hank? Who's doing this?" Bill's voice grew louder and more intense. "What happened? Do they know yet?"

"They're not sure yet," Hank replied. "It looks like he was burned alive in his chair, but the reason is still unknown. Fires have a nasty habit of destroying most of the helpful evidence."

"Crap, Hank. We need to tell the others. We need to warn them. What if they're next?"

"I agree," Hank said. "I'm going to have to do this unofficially, though. I haven't been invited to investigate any of these murders, so until I have a solid case to present to my superior, what I'm doing needs to stay very quiet."

"What can I do?" Bill asked. His voice was stronger this time.

Hank thought for a moment. "Call the others. They need to hear your story, and the rest of the details, too. I know it's short notice, but ask them to meet at your place today at 3:00 p.m. We'll lay it all out for them."

"Okay, that sounds good," Bill said. "I'll make the calls and see you then."

"Take care, Bill. Watch your back and lock your doors."

With that, Hank hung up. Then, placing the phone into one of the car's cup-holders, he brought his large hands up to his face and began to weep.

* * *

Steve poured the hot coffee into both mugs and carried them to the table. Beth would be down from the shower any moment and he liked having her morning caffeine fix ready for her when she arrived. His, black with a touch of sugar, and hers with milk.

Their mornings were fairly routine, a benefit of having small children. Each morning, weekday and weekend alike, followed the same pattern and offered the same small window to talk and catch up.

Beth had returned the night before while he had been standing outside, apparently out past the property line and in the wetlands behind the house. He remembered walking up to the house by the light of her headlights and meeting her at the door to the kitchen. His slippers had been thoroughly soaked in dark, pungent water from the marsh.

His jeans, though, were what had alarmed him. The wetness stopped just a few inches above his knees, meaning that he had, without knowing it, nearly drown himself. The soil in the wetlands behind his house was notoriously similar to quicksand, and hikers were frequently warned to avoid the salt marshes that dotted the coastline of Cape Ann. The mixture of changing tides and dangerous footing could be deadly.

Steve was thankful he had come to his senses when he had, but he was more frightened by the fact that he had lost them in the first place. Between that and apparently forgetting to shut the door to the girls' room, there was a lot about the previous evening that concerned him.

"Morning," Beth said from the doorway. She was smiling at him, and it warmed his soul.

"Well, hello there," he replied, smiling back. "Coffee?"

"Gladly," she said, and took a seat across from him at the table. "So, ready to talk about last night?"

Steve frowned. She had tried to get the story out of him after it had happened, but he wasn't able to offer her much. He was pretty sure she had assumed he was drunk, and let it go for the time being, but now she wanted to know what had happened and he had no choice but to offer what little explanation he could.

"There's not much to talk about, really," he replied. "Honestly."

"Steve, I caught you walking through the back yard last night. It was black as pitch out there, and you were soaked to the bone. I know you're a little slow in the morning, but don't you think recreational hikes through the wetlands in the dark are a bit odd?"

"You're a comedian, and so early in the morning, too. I'm a lucky guy."

"I'm serious, Steve." She sounded more annoyed this time. "What the hell happened last night?"

He sighed and looked at his hands. "I'm not sure, honey. I have vague memories of being in the house. Something about lights outside, and this intense desire to go find them."

"Lights? You mean, like someone in the yard with a flashlight?"

"No, not like that." He struggled for the right words. "If I close my eyes I can still see them. Almost like fireflies, but more cool and faint. Maybe more round too, if that makes sense?"

"And, what, you just decided to go chasing lights?" She sounded both vexed and amused. "I don't get it, Steve. What was the draw?"

"I'm telling you, Beth, I don't know." He took a sip of his coffee and then blew on it, trying to cool it off. "I felt...I don't know...I felt drawn to them. It was like a voice in my head, whispering to go find them. I must have wandered out in the middle of that. I don't remember much until you came home."

Beth was quiet for a moment, staring off toward the sink and the window over it. Steve took another sip of his coffee, and then, when he discovered it was cool enough, took a full drink.

"You know, this is going to sound crazy," she began, "but I've heard of something like this before."

"Oh?" He followed her gaze toward the window and took another drink.

"My friend Linda, the one who works some of the same shifts with me at the store, was chatting with me just the other day. We were cleaning up in the back room and the topic of George's funeral came up. I mentioned how sad it was and how hard it must be for parents to lose an adult child. We were chatting about how inadequate the funeral process is in helping people deal with death."

"I can understand that," Steve said. "It's a lot more helpful for building a social gathering for the mourners, but I have to wonder if it's what people like George's parents really need right now. At the end of the afternoon, Stephen and Maggie still had to go home alone, right. And the whole process can be over and done in just a couple of days. That must be frightening; the world moves on and you're left to grieve on your own, without help."

Beth nodded. "That's why I've always loved the idea of the Jewish mourning process. For the seven days after the funeral, all of the immediate family gathers in one home and they spend that time together. They call it *sitting shiva*—the Hebrew word for seven—and it really gives them time to process and mourn as a community. It's beautiful."

"It sounds healthy, too. But what does it have to do with Linda?"

"Oh," she replied, "nothing really, I guess. I got off track. No, Linda is part American Indian, and she was telling me how many of the ancient burial practices of her ancestors are still followed. Things that sounds so much more helpful and intentional."

"Like what?" He took a long drink and looked back at her.

"Oh, they do things like blackening their faces as a sign to others that they're mourning. A lot of what they do seems counter-intuitive, such as wearing unpresentable clothing, rather than getting all dressed up. They even wear their hair down."

"Man, I hate dressing up for funerals. That sounds amazing."

"No kidding. Deciding what to wear to a funeral is horrible. 'Will I look good in this? Too good? Is it disrespectful to look bad?' I practically need therapy after picking out clothes for a funeral."

Steve chuckled. "I hear you. So, take this back to the lights. That's where you were going, right?"

"Oh, right." She took a long drink of her coffee. "So Linda was sharing other stories that she felt might entertain me. One local legend is about something they call the *tepay wanka* or something like that. I'm bad with other languages. Anyway, some people call them *will-o-wisps*, or spirit lights, and they are supposed to be otherworldly."

"The lights, you mean?"

"Yeah, she said that there are demons that use the lights as bait to lure people to their deaths. Then, the souls of those people are added to the lights, and the process repeats. I could be remembering it wrong, but I think it was something close to that."

"So you think that I was coaxed outside last night by some Native American demon and its spirit lights?" Steve chuckled softly. "And you thought *I* was drunk," he added with a smile.

"At least I have a theory, sweetheart. You've got nothing more than a foggy dream about pretty lights and swimming in the back yard."

Steve checked his watch and then pushed his chair back and stood up. "Well, it's something to think about, I suppose. But it's almost 7:30 and I've got to get to work."

He leaned over and kissed her. "Thanks for the chat. I'll let you know if I remember anything else."

He took his mug over to the sink and rinsed it out, and then glanced out the window. There was fog over the marsh now, and no lights to be seen, but the view still gave him a chill. He turned to head toward the door, but stopped when he felt his phone vibrate in his pocket.

"Who could I morning?" he asked

"Maybe an ei
He looked at
McCarthy." He gave
furrowed and head c

"Hey Bill, wh.
"Did I catch y
"Nope, just he
up?"

Bill paused, ar
had been dropped, bu
friend started talking

"Roger is dead
this morning. It happe

Last night, Steve
Beth sat up str
contact with him. Her

to know more, but he held up a hand to ask her to wait.

"He was burned in his apartment, apparently. Hank doesn't think it was an accident."

"What?" The news was just too incredible to believe. First George, and now Roger? That didn't make sense. The odds were too long. He felt afraid and concerned and incredibly sad. "Why would someone—"

Bill cut him off. "There's a lot to talk about, but Hank thinks all of us should get together to do that in person. Can you get out of work early today and get over to my place by 3:00 p.m.?"

"I...yeah...I'll make it work." He tossed another glance toward Beth. "Yeah, I'll be there."

"Great. Okay, man. Stay safe today, and get here as soon as you can. There's a lot to talk about."

"Alright," he replied. "See you then."

He hung up the call and looked back at Beth.

"Honey, what happened?" she asked, her voice full of concern.

"Roger is dead," he said with disbelief. "He was murdered."

CHAPTER ELEVEN

Mike couldn't concentrate. His email inbox was quickly filling up with messages from his team, and the phone kept ringing with calls from his supervisor. There was a growing stack of paperwork in the basket at the corner of his desk and Brenda, his secretary, kept bringing more in. He couldn't think straight; his mind was entirely focused on the call he had received from Bill earlier that morning. Roger, another of his old childhood friends, was dead.

He had, of course, already found a dozen reasons why Roger's death was his fault. Mike was good at that. He excelled at that. If Harvard offered a Ph.D program in self-blame, he would graduate summa cum laude and they would name a building after him. He was gifted, that was certain.

Of course, like most artists, he saw his gift as a curse, because that's what it truly was. So here he sat in the privacy of his office, consumed by thoughts of guilt and shame. His only other option was to allow the fear that sat outside the door of his mind to enter in and overtake him. Mike didn't handle fear too well, though.

Bill said that Roger had been murdered, and after connecting the dots to the murder of George Ashcroft, Mike was left with a very bad feeling. It would be easy to assume their deaths were connected. And maybe that's what Hank and Bill wanted to talk about. Perhaps they *were* connected in some way. And if those two deaths were related, then what did that mean for the rest of them?

The only work call he had placed all morning was to his supervisor to let him know that he would be leaving early today to handle some personal matters. He didn't elaborate—he wasn't even sure if he could, given the circumstances—and his boss didn't ask him to. In fact, he seemed disinterested.

He wondered how productive he was really going to be over the next few hours, though, regardless of his early dismissal. Unless he wanted to share his fear and guilt with every member of his accounting team, as well as Brenda—a woman unanimously recognized as the reigning champion of office gossip—he had to face the fact that his office would have to keep moving without him.

Instead, he turned inward and allowed himself to marinate in the guilt that came so naturally to him. The fact that three of the seven men he grew up with had now died was causing him to acknowledge his own mortality. The allure of reviewing expense budgets for a dozen small businesses had become all but nonexistent.

Work, like so many things he knew, had become dead to him.

* * *

Steve was the last to arrive at Bill's house just after 3:00 p.m. that afternoon. He managed to find a parking spot on the street, an accomplishment that could be difficult because of how close Chestnut Street was to downtown Salem. Parking on side streets like this one filled up quickly with cars from tourist and commuters, only thinning out again after dinner.

The view down the street was striking. Both sides were lined with trees that still held most of their brilliant orange, yellow and red leaves. It was beautiful against the backdrop of the large red brick manors with their black wrought-iron fencing. Steve thought it looked like a Norman Rockwell painting.

Bill greeted him at the door and led him inside. The study was just past a large living room and a small butler's pantry tucked behind the staircase. Steve had trouble finding space in his own home for a place to set whatever book he was currently reading, due to all the toys and child-proofing Beth had enacted years ago. Bill clearly didn't have this issue, judging by the large swaths of square footage that he occupied all by himself.

The others were gathered near the fireplace in Bill's office, a room which he called his study even though it more closely resembled a private library. On the far wall, in front of a wide window, was a small walnut desk with Bill's laptop perched on it like a historical anomaly. Centered in the wall nearest the doorway was a fireplace wide enough to roast an entire lamb, making the small pile of unlit firewood seem like a parody.

It was the rest of the space that was truly impressive. The wall to either side of the fireplace, as well as the two side walls, were covered with bookshelves that spanned the distance from floor to ceiling. Each polished wooden shelf was completely filled with the spines of the thousands of books that comprised Bill's collection, and it was spectacular to behold.

"Hey Steve," said Mike as he walked into the room. The men shook hands quickly. "Good to see you again."

"I wish it was for a better reason, though," Steve replied. He looked around at the others in the room, and their faces seemed to echo this sentiment. None were smiling, and Mike even seemed on the verge of despair, though that didn't surprise him.

"Alright gentlemen," Hank interrupted from his seat at the end of a large leather sofa. "Let's get to it."

Steve grabbed a seat in an armchair near the sofa and leaned forward, elbows on his knees. "What's going on, Hank? Roger was killed? I can't believe it."

"It's true," the detective replied. "I wish it wasn't, trust me, but it is. But there's more to the story, and I think it might be best if we back up and cover some other details first."

"What details?" asked Mike. "You mean George?"

"Maybe," interjected Bill from behind the sofa. He stepped around to stand near Hank. "I think I'll start with George, but there might be earlier things to mention. We'll get to that."

"Please, after you, Mr. Fancy Writer," Hank wryly beckoned with an outstretched hand.

"I'll see what I can do," he said, and then took a deep breath. "Hank did some digging around in the investigation of George's death. I mean that literally; he went to Dogtown and poked around in a professional capacity. And he discovered that what George's dad told us at the funeral was only part of the truth."

"Stephen was lying to us?" Mike asked.

"No, not at all," Bill replied. "It just seems that he wasn't given all of the pieces. The truth of what happened to George was, shall we say, censored."

Hank leaned forward to interrupt. "Before you all get your panties in a bunch, this is fairly common, and wisely so. It's standard procedure. If there is evidence that might cause an investigation more harm than good, it's routinely withheld until all the questions have been answered."

"I get it," said Steve. "Like when the police know the identity of a suspect, but they don't tell the newspapers because they want to sneak up and catch the guy, right?"

Hank laughed. "Well, it's not as dramatic as television would have you believe, but yeah, that's the nut of it."

"So, what did you learn?" Mike asked.

"Well, for one thing," Bill replied, "we learned that the police missed some key evidence. Hank followed the drag marks that were made when the killer moved George's body in front of the boulder from the woods—another detail they neglected to mention to the Ashcrofts—and found some odd fibers in the trees."

"Fibers?" Steve said.

"More like hairs," Hank replied. "Honestly, they look like quills."

"You mean, as in the kind of needles on the back of a porcupine?"

"Exactly like them," Bill replied. "But we'll get back to that in a moment. The next thing to mention is that I was attacked in my back yard the night of the funeral. We had all gone out for a drink, remember, and then I drove Roger home."

"Who attacked you?" Steve asked. "Or what?"

"I can answer this one," Mike said. "Bill came over shortly after it happened. The short story is that he heard noises in the bushes at the back of his yard, and when he inspected them he found his neighbor's dog dead with its head ripped off."

"Whoa." Steve recoiled at the thought. "The head was gone?"

Bill nodded. "And right after finding it, I saw something in the bushes. There were...eyes...red eyes...and I ran." He swallowed hard, the emotions of that night rushing back. "I had my back to it when it attacked me. I never saw it, but Mike and I have had a working theory that it was a coyote."

"A theory I find to be very, very wrong," Hank added.

"How so?" asked Mike. This denial was news to him. "Did you call animal control like I suggested?"

"Yep," Bill replied with a weak grin. "They told me to call the police, but I called Hank, instead."

"You'll never guess what I found when I checked out the area where the dog was found." He paused and waited for someone to take a stab at the answer, but no one did. "Quills. More of the same damn quills."

"Hold on a minute," Mike said. He was shaking his head, as if the details were having trouble fitting into his mind. "Why would there be—"

Steve cut him off. "They're connected!" he shouted, jumping to his feet at the same time.

"That's my working theory," Hank said. "And it gets easier to accept it when you learn about what I found in Roger's apartment near the place where he was burned alive in a big arm chair."

"Oh, damn," said Mike with a sigh. "What a horrible way to die. I can't believe...man, poor Roger."

"What did you find?" Steve asked, slowly retaking his seat in the chair. "Wait, I bet I know: more quills, right?"

Hank nodded. "Just one, but I don't think finding a handful would have made the connection any more solid. I think we have irrefutable proof that whoever was behind George's death was also behind the attack on Bill, and now Roger's death. The Salem police are calling it an accidental death for now, but I think the full evidence points to something more sinister."

"Which leads us back to Dogtown," Bill added. "The Gloucester police withheld something else from us. But Hank was able to pull some strings and get a better picture of what they know."

"Can I ask a question?" Mike interrupted.

"Shoot," said Hank with a nod.

"Why aren't you taking this investigation to your department? I mean, shouldn't this be something more official than a few friends trading details around the proverbial fire?"

"You want me to go to my Captain and tell him that I snooped in on a local investigation—because I was personally connected to the victim, mind you—and that I had found porcupine quills? I would then have to explain that I had found the same quills at the scene of two other crimes. If I did that, I'm not sure if he would laugh or suspend me. Probably both."

Mike nodded slowly. "Sorry. I guess I didn't think that one through all the way, did I?"

"No worries," Hank replied. "It's hard to predict how a superior officer might take something like this, even if you work with him. I'm pretty sure my Captain would clean my clock and send me packing. He's a hard-ass."

"So what'd you learn?" asked Steve, bringing the conversation back on track.

"He learned," Bill answered, "that the message on the boulder, the one where George's body had been found, was censored by the police. The Ashcrofts had been given only part of it."

"Remind me again what Stephen told us it said," Steve said.

"He told us it said 'SAVE YOURSELF', using the SAVE that was already engraved on it, and the additional words written in George's blood. But Hank learned that there were three more words after that message."

"It said 'SAVE YOURSELF, ALL OF YOU'" Hank said.

Quiet fell on the room. The men looked around at each other in silence, processing the message and working through its implications. Then Bill spoke up.

"Guys, you see what's happening, don't you?" He paused and looked around, making eye contact with each of the others. Hank nodded grimly, while Mike and Steve stewed in the horror of this revelation. "We—our small group of childhood friends that began as seven—is being picked off by some crazed, unknown killer."

"Wait, *seven*? Kenny died twenty years ago, Bill." Steve seemed confused. "His death isn't connected to these new ones. It couldn't be."

"No," Hank jumped in, "but our association to each other is the thread that connects the two recent murders, as well as the attack on Bill, which we can safely guess was a failed attempt by the same individual. We have to assume, then, that the rest of us are targets as well."

"Someone we all know?" Mike pondered out loud. "Someone connected to the accident at Clements?"

"I have no idea," replied Bill. "Again, Hank and I are just working through the theories that have the best chance of making sense. For now, it seems like there's someone who's got it out for all of us."

"I had a weird experience last night," Steve said, seemingly at random. Everyone stopped and turned to him. "I don't know what to do with it, but maybe full disclosure would help."

The other three men sat quietly and listened to Steve's retelling of the events of the previous evening, beginning with the mysteriously open door to the room his daughter's sleep in, all the way up to Beth's arrival and how she found him returning from a dangerous walk in the marsh.

There was a moment when he considered stopping there, but something in his wife's story of the lights felt important to mention. He skipped the details about funerals, even though he knew that most of the others would appreciate hearing about it on a personal level.

Instead, he told them about the American Indian stories of the demon who lures people to their deaths with lights.

"I'm not sure what to do with that," Bill said in response. "But I think the lesson we're learning here is that all of the details, even the ones that seem unrelated, are potentially helpful to finding the answer. That said, I'm glad you're alright, Steve."

"Likewise," said Hank.

"Hey, guys?" Steve said quickly, and then he jumped back to his feet. "I know this will sound crazy, but what if this person—the killer, whoever they are—has included Kenny's dad on the list, since Kenny himself isn't here to be killed?"

"That's the stupidest thing I've heard all afternoon," Mike said without looking Steve in the eye.

"No, I think he's on to something," Hank replied. "There's very little to connect all of us besides our friendship, and that's rooted in a time when Kenny was with us. In fact, am I wrong in assuming that we stopped being that tight group of friends right after his death? Is that even fair to say?"

"No, I can own up to my own part in that," Mike said guiltily. "It was hard to look at you guys after he died. You were all a daily reminder of what happened."

"Yeah," Steve said. "I went through a bit of that, myself. We drifted apart. It happens to good friends, and we had Kenny's death to make it happen more quickly, I suppose."

"I agree," Bill added. "Was doing that fair to each other? Probably not. But was it a natural response? I think so."

"Alright," continued Hank, "so if someone is angry with us, enough to want all of us dead, then they must be angry about something from that period of time, at or around the time of Kenny's death."

"Hell, maybe it has nothing to do with the accident," Bill added.

"How do you figure?" Hank replied.

"The quills." He waited for Hank to catch on, but the detective seemed oblivious. "Remember I told you I saw something at Dogtown when we were kids? Something with quills?"

"Right," Hank replied. "Sorry, that's probably not as significant of a memory for me as it is for you."

"Do you remember who drove us there to Dogtown that day?"

Mike interrupted with the answer first. "Kenny's dad!"

"Right!" Bill affirmed. "What if all of us—us seven kids plus Kenny's dad—violated something...unnatural. Hell, I don't know. But isn't it worth considering that it all started there?"

"Absolutely," Hank replied. "That's a strong case, Bill. Well done."

"And that means Mr. Tobey might be on the list, too," Steve added.

Hank nodded. "I think that's a fair assumption."

"Then I'm going to go check on him," Steve said. He was already headed toward the door. "He needs to be warned, at the very least."

"Be careful, Steve," Hank called after him. "And come back when you're done. We've got some group decisions to make."

Steve nodded and then disappeared out into the hall. A moment later the others heard the front door shut. Bill walked over to the cabinet.

"I need a drink. Does anyone else want one?"

"I'll take some of that Glenlivet, if you're offering," said Hank, glancing over the back of the sofa.

"I'm good. Thanks, though," said Mike.

"What do you guys think about Steve's story, the one about the spirit lights?" asked Hank.

Bill stopped pouring the drink into a short glass tumbler, and looked up at his friend. "You mean, do I think that there is something supernatural going on here?"

Hank nodded. "I'm willing to put all the options on the table at this point."

Mike laughed. "You've got to be kidding me," he said. "Are you guys telling me that you're actually going to consider ghost stories?"

"No, I'm just asking," Hank replied. "Let's talk things through. Who else could be interested in killing us? I mean, whoever it is has managed to kill George and Roger, and even though they screwed it up, we can be sure that Bill was a target too. That makes it pretty obvious that the rest of us are on the list. So who's behind it?"

Mike thought for a moment and then spoke up. "I have an idea, but you guys aren't going to like it much."

Bill came back over and handed a glass to Hank before sitting down. "Spit it out," he said. "Let's hear it."

"Mr. Tobey," he said flatly, and the moment the words rolled off his tongue he wondered if he had stepped out of line. "I realize Steve is lumping him in as a possible victim. But why? What if this is about Kenny's death. He's not responsible for that. That'd be us. We're to blame, right?"

Hank nodded in agreement. Bill seemed to be waiting for more proof.

"And Mr. Tobey isn't responsible for the destruction of that old mill building, either, right? I mean, that was us. We caused the accident. We're the ones to blame. And I think Mr. Tobey is the one who is blaming us."

"Mike," Bill began. "I think you're jumping—" but Mike cut him off.

"I know," he said to Bill's unspoken question. "I know I blame myself for everything. It's what I do. Yeah, it's probably an issue I should get sorted out, but on this I'm right: Kenny's death and the accident were entirely our fault. If anyone has a reason to be pissed at us for what happened, that person is Kenny's father."

The three men sat in silence for a moment as their words settled around them like dust. Bill looked at his glass again, but it was empty and he couldn't remember finishing it off, so he set it down. Hank's eyes connected with his.

"Why now?" Hank asked. "I mean, all of that happened twenty years ago. Why now?"

Mike was the first to answer. "George saw him right before he died."

"What?" Hank and Bill said in unison.

"Yeah," he continued. "I saw George at the Midtown right before he was killed. He bumped into me on the way out and said he'd just seen Kenny's dad inside. The thought of seeing him scared me out of my mind, so I decided to skip the coffee and leave. A few days later, George was dead."

Bill was beginning to see it now, too. "The next time he saw any of us, it was at the funeral when we were all there together. The attacks started right after that. Yes!"

"So you guys are saying that he didn't try to kill us for two decades because he hadn't seen us?" Hank seemed to be having a difficult time believing it was that simple. "That the moment he knew we were alive—what we looked like or where we lived or something benign—he had what he needed? Guys, that's just a little, I don't know, weak."

"How so?" asked Bill. "It makes sense to me. Think of it this way: imagine that Mr. Tobey has some sort of vendetta with us because of what happened. He loses touch with us for years. Heck, maybe it took years for him to realize just how angry he really was. Maybe it was seeing George in the café that flipped the last switch in his mind, setting him into action. I mean, the guy lost his only child, right? Desperate people sometimes seem crazy when they act on that desperation, but to them it makes perfect sense."

"So why hasn't he tried to kill me, or Mike?" Hank asked.

"You guys are probably the hardest to find alone. You're a police officer, making you a less than ideal target, and Mike is a workaholic who practically lives at his office, mostly around other people."

"Hey, that hurts," Mike replied. "But yeah, it's true."

"See? Roger, though, he lived alone in a quiet apartment building. George was alone hiking in the woods when he was killed. I live by myself here, and got caught outside in the dark without anyone else around. And Steve was alone when he was lured outside last night."

Bill stopped, frozen in place. The others looked at him, unsure what had happened.

"What?" Hank said. "Bill, what is it?"

Bill was quiet for a moment longer, and then he stood up and headed for the door.

"Steve!" he shouted at them. "Steve went to check on Kenny's dad thirty minutes ago."

"Dammit," Hank said, jumping to his feet. He moved quickly after Bill, with Mike following close behind. "Come on. I'll drive."

CHAPTER TWELVE

Steve pulled onto the street where Kenny's father still lived and memories began to wash over him. It had been many years since he had travelled down this street, but even though there were differences, the essence of the neighborhood remained the same.

This area of Hollesley had been built up in the late 1950s and had been targeted toward the wealthier home owner. That translated into wider lots, plenty of trees and privacy, and homes that had a bit of a modern flare. Some of the homes still retained their original charm and condition, but many were tired, worn-out versions of what the builders had intended.

Kenny rarely hosted activities that the group had planned. Sleepovers usually happened at Mike's house because his parents had finished their basement and filled it with all the things that kept kids busy and happy, such as a ping-pong table and a computer for games. Outdoor adventures typically started at Bill's house due to its proximity to the river and the park. Hank's parents, on the other hand, had an incredibly large yard for the kids to play sports.

The only times that Steve remembered coming anywhere near Kenny's house was when they carpooled home from one of the other houses. Since Kenny's dad was a single father, the burden usually fell to Steve's mom to drive the gang home, so most of his memories of Kenny's house were just views from the driveway.

He slowed his car to a crawl and scanned the mailboxes as he passed them. The afternoon light was failing fast and it was becoming harder to pick the letters out in the dusk. The names he saw, though, began to sound familiar. Madson, then Rodriguez, followed by Jamieson. Then he saw a driveway appear on his right and knew he had arrived.

The drive was bordered on both sides by dying pines, their yellow needles covering the dirt on either side of the broken blacktop. A mailbox was perched on top of a dark green post that looked as if it hadn't been painted in decades. The numbers on the side of the box were still just as legible as they had been in middle school, though.

Steve turned his car into the drive and started down the short path to the house. It was set deep into the property, and most of the front yard was filled with large rocks and tall pine trees. It made the house difficult to find, even on a clear day, until rounding the last little curve revealed its location.

The house hadn't aged well. The cedar siding had faded from the bright, earthy yellow of Steve's childhood memories to a pale gray streaked with darker stains beneath the sills and along the roofline. The lawn was unkept and one of the shutters had come loose, causing it to hang at an odd angle. The house didn't look abandoned, but it certainly seemed forgotten.

The structure spread outward from the left side of the driveway, beginning with a large two-car garage. There was an old Bronco in front of one of the garage doors, and Steve couldn't help but wonder if it was the same one he had taken rides in as a boy. It certainly looked old enough to have been the same truck.

He parked beside the Bronco and got out of his car. The scent of pine was intoxicating, but there was also a hint of something rancid in the air. Steve assumed it was a dead animal in the bushes behind the garage and headed toward the front door.

He found it was amazing that he had never actually stood on this front porch, but here he was, viewing the door for the first time in his life. He reached up and rapped his knuckles on the peeling wood and then waited for a response.

The yard was quiet, and something about that seemed out of place. He turned and looked at the high branches of the old pines. Everything looked as empty as it sounded. It was as if nothing alive remained in the area. *Early migration habits fooled by the Indian summer, perhaps?* He wasn't an expert in the science of ecology or a student of wildlife, so he admitted his ignorance and accepted it.

He heard a rustling sound from behind the door and then it opened, revealing a dimly-lit room and a familiar face. It was Daniel Tobey.

"Mr. Tobey," he started, but the door opened wider as is friend's father flashed a smile.

"Steve," he said cheerfully. "What a surprise. Come on inside." The man moved back and Steve stepped through the doorway.

Steve smiled and offered his hand. Daniel closed the door and then shook it. "Good to see you well, Mr. Tobey," he said.

"Please," he said. "We're both adults. Daniel is fine. "Here, let's go into the kitchen. There's more light there, and it's a lot less of a disaster than the rest of the house." Both of the men chuckled.

The kitchen was just past the living room, past a waist-high wall that ended with a post that reached all the way to the ceiling. Piles of mail and paperwork littered the floor, and magazines were stacked neatly on the half-wall.

Steve took a seat at the table just inside the dinning area. The tabletop was a large, dusty rectangle of blue-green glass. Its edges and corners had been beveled, and the entire sheet of glass rested on a dark steel frame that felt very modern compared to the rest of the house.

"So, to what do I owe your unexpected visit?" Daniel asked.

"Well, it's not the greatest news," Steve began, "but I felt that you needed to know what was going on. The police found Roger O'Connor dead this morning in his apartment."

Daniel visibly tensed and then took a deep breath. "Oh, that's horrible," he said. He looked pained and distressed. "How sad, Steve. Can I ask how? Do they know what happened?"

"They aren't sure yet, to be honest. The police say that it appears he burned to death while sitting in a chair in his living room, but they've found no evidence of arson. To be honest, Daniel, I think they're looking at it as an accident. Hank, though, thinks it might be murder."

"Murder? Oh my," the older man said with a sigh. "What a horrible idea."

Daniel looked down at his hands for a moment and Steve waited for the right moment to press forward. Finally he managed to make eye contact with the man. *Is that anger in his eyes?* he thought.

"There's more," he finally said.

Daniel looked stricken. "More?" His voice was that of a wounded man. Steve wondered how much of the pain he was feeling right now was a reliving of the pain he felt when he lost Kenny.

"Bill was attacked by something on Saturday evening after coming home from the funeral. We aren't positive yet, but Hank and Bill are pretty convinced that the deaths of George and Roger, as well as this attack on Bill, are all connected."

"Connected?" the older man asked. "How could that be?"

"We—that's Mike, Bill, Hank and myself—think that there's someone behind all of it. Someone who's upset with us, who wants revenge or something. I'm not sure I understand it all myself, but that's the working theory right now."

"Connected," he said, his voice trailing off. Daniel stood and walked toward the large patio door behind him. For a few moments there was no sound. He just seemed to stare off into the back yard, lost in his thoughts.

"Mr. Tobey," he began, and then corrected himself. "Sorry. Daniel. We were thinking that if we're on some sort of list of targets, perhaps you might be as well. I came over to warn you, to ask you to be careful."

The man didn't turn around, but Steve could hear his breathing. It was no longer slow and steady, but more deep and labored. Then a vibration on his hip broke his concentration. He pulled his phone out and read the short text message that had come from Bill's number.

The killer is Daniel. Don't go near him. We are coming.

He looked up. Daniel had turned around to face him.

Steve noticed that the man's eyes looked narrower, more dark and piercing. There was an anger and hate behind them that almost knocked him back. When the older man spoke, his voice chilled Steve to the bone.

"I wondered how long it would take you to come scratching at my door like a frightened dog." His voice was a venomous hiss and his face was twisted, as if in agony. "Do you think I'm going to let you stop me? They were foolish to send you alone."

Steve stood up, toppling the chair in his haste. "Wait," he muttered. *Stupid!* he cursed at himself. *Why did I come here alone? And how did he know?*

Thinking as fast as he could, he lied.

"I'm not alone." His words came out rigid with panic. Daniel stepped closer to him, his hands balled into tight fists. "Mike is in the car. He's going to call the others if I don't come back outside."

"Liar!" the man shouted. "You're nothing but a liar. I should never have let you near my son. You and the rest are all bad seeds. You killed my boy."

Steve stumbled backwards, but he collided with the half-wall that divided the living room from the kitchen, knocking a stack of magazines to the floor. His heart was racing and his body was flooding with adrenaline, but there was nowhere to go.

"You're alone, Stephen," hissed Daniel. "All alone. Yes, and you are outnumbered, too. You're alone, but I am not, you see."

Daniel pointed into the other room, and Steve turned to see what he meant. His mind struggled to process what he saw standing in the living room, though. The room was more dim than the kitchen and the shadows seemed to be toying with his vision. But fear began to creep up his spine and fill his gut with rotten chills.

A figure stood in the center of the living room. It was about half the height of a man and was wrapped in faded brown cloth. The creature—for it wasn't human, that much was clear—had skin that was a pale gray, appearing almost ghostly in the dim light. And it was staring back at him.

Steve screamed and backed away from it, but struck the table with his hip. The creature's face was a mass of exaggerated features. Its nose was too long and the ears seemed to be pointy, cutting through the strands of matted hair like dorsal fins. Around it all, like a halo radiating from behind its head, were thin, pale quills protruding from its back and shoulders.

Steve saw them, and the puzzle snapped into place in his mind. Quills. Not from a porcupine, but from this hideous thing. Is this what George saw as he took his final breath? Would Roger have known that it was this thing that ended his life?

Its thin lips were pulled back in a cruel grin, exposing dozens of tiny, razor-sharp teeth. They were covered in crimson, as if it had been drinking something dark and thick, and a thin, serpent-like tongue flitted behind them. It was the creature's eyes that frightened Steve the most, though. They were locked on his own, and he felt pinned down and trapped by their red gaze.

"Say hello to one of my helpers," Daniel said from somewhere behind him, though Steve wasn't sure if the older man was introducing him to the creature, or the other way around. "I think you two will get along nicely."

The creature flashed a hungry, evil grin at him, and one last guttural scream escaped Steve's lips.

Then it was upon him, and his world become a storm of pain and darkness.

* * *

Hank was pushing his car as fast as he could manage through the small streets of Hollesley, cutting through neighborhoods to avoid the evening traffic in the town center. The sun had begun to set a few minutes earlier as they entered town, and now they were all squinting out the windows at the street signs, looking for the road that led to Daniel Tobey's house.

As soon as the trio had pulled away from Bill's house in Salem, they had begun a heated discussion of what they needed to do next. Hank insisted that it wouldn't be a simple matter to call the police. There was no evidence, outside of the few quills that they themselves had gathered, that connected the deaths, and only one of them was being treated as a murder case. No, quick results wouldn't be possible, Hank was certain.

Time was quickly escaping them, and if Steve was still alive, every moment they spent trying to convince the local police to believe their story was a moment that could be used to save him. Hank knew it might end his career if the next hour went badly, but their only hope was to save their friend and stop a killer, and only then would they have the freedom to explain everything to the authorities.

Bill had sent a message to Steve as soon as they climbed into the car, warning him about Kenny's father and telling him that they were on their way to join him. Steve hadn't replied, however, and that sat very uneasily with all of them. Something was wrong, and they were powerless to help him until they arrived.

"There!" Mike yelled, pointing at the green sign at the corner. "Take a left here, and I think the house is farther down on the right."

Hank spun the steering wheel and the car rounded the corner without decelerating. The tires cried out in agony as the car skidded across the intersection, nearly colliding with a utility pole before enough momentum was lost to allow them to pull ahead.

"Easy, Hank!" Bill screamed from the back seat. "We're no good to Steve if we roll the car into a neighbor's house."

Hank wasn't talking, though. He had gone unusually quiet, and all of his focus seemed to be poured into the operation of the car, practically willing it toward their destination. He sat slightly hunched, his eyes scanning the dark signs and mailboxes as they sped down the road.

"Here it is. Stop!" Mike put both hands on the dash to brace himself, and Hank stomped on the brake as hard as he could. Mike pointed to the driveway on their right, and the car lurched forward and raced down the winding path.

They reached the house in a matter of seconds and found Steve's car parked in front of the right-side garage door. A motion light mounted above on the garage flickered on, illuminating both vehicles. Hank killed the engine and bolted from the car as fast as he could. Bill didn't see his friend unholster his service weapon, but there was a large handgun in Hank's grip as he approached the other vehicle.

Mike and Bill followed quickly after their friend, but allowed him to lead the search due to his experience and training. While Hank was peering in through the windows, the other men stayed back near the black Ford and watched.

"Nothing," Hank barked. "He's not in the car."

Bill nodded, but Mike pointed to the driveway beside the abandoned car. The others followed his gesture and instantly saw what he had. Smeared across the pale concrete of the driveway, now visible in the bright light from the garage, was a trail of blood.

"Oh, man," Bill muttered, unable to stop looking at it.

Hank let out a fierce growl before sprinting toward the front door. The others followed him as fast as they could, but by the time they had reached the door, Hank had already kicked it in and was clearing the room carefully from the doorway.

"It's empty," he said quietly. "No one's here."

"Steve!" shouted Mike. "Hey man, are you in here?" Nothing but silence returned to their ears.

The three men stepped inside the house. Bill found the light switch and flipped it, illuminating the havoc that the darkness had hidden. Furniture was toppled across the living room floor and the kitchen table on the far side of the house—apparently one with a glass top—had been shattered into a pile of small blue-green shards.

There was also blood. More blood than Mike or Bill had ever seen. The air was heavy with the acrid, metallic scent of it, and Bill could feel bile rising in his throat. He cast a glance at Mike, who had a hand across his own mouth and nose. Neither appeared to be handling it well.

Hank, however, had seen his fair share of gore in his years of service, and was unfazed by the scene. He moved carefully across the living room toward the pool of blood that marked the entrance to the kitchen area, casting his gaze around the room as he did so. While he was careful not to disturb anything that might help investigators later, he still moved quickly.

Mike lagged behind the others as they crossed the living room. He stopped to look at a jacket that Daniel had left draped over the back of a chair. It wasn't the same brown coat he has seen the older man wearing the other day at the cafe, but it had the same dusty appearance.

He touched the material and then looked at the tip of his finger. The dust was fine and powdery, but clearly debris from something solid. Most dust in a house was the microscopic dander and dead skin that blew away in a small breeze, but this was more substantial.

It reminded Mike of the summers he spent in college working for a remodeling contractor, installing windows in old homes. He would come home every evening covered in the gritty dust from sheet rock and wood. It seemed to spread and get onto everything he owned, like a virus in a kindergarten class.

"Don't touch anything," Hank said firmly from the kitchen. He was peering around the corner at Mike, and motioned his free hand toward the jacket. "Whoever processes this scene later is going to need that evidence, and you probably don't want them finding your prints here, do you?"

Mike pulled his hand back as if it had been bitten, and then brushed the dust off his fingers. He joined up with Bill, who was standing on the living room side of the half-wall that separated the kitchen from the rest of the house. Bill was nudging at a pile of magazines on the floor with his foot, and had exposed the cover of one of the issues deeper in the stack.

"*Renovation Monthly?*" Bill muttered as Mike approached. "I had no idea he was a carpenter."

"Not in the strictest sense of the word," Mike replied. "He's a handyman from what I've heard. Not a full-blown contractor, though."

"Guys," Hank interrupted. "I'm going to take a look at the rest of the house. I'm fairly certain we're alone in here, but I don't want to take the chances that we passed right over Steve's location and missed him."

"Sure thing," Bill said. "What would you like us to do?"

Hank smiled wryly. "Just stay there and don't touch anything."

"Yes, dad," Mike quipped sarcastically.

"Bite me, Mikey," Hank replied, and then walked off slowly down the hall that led to the rest of the house, gun held out and ready.

Bill stepped back toward the living room and scanned the area for anything that might be worth noticing. The furniture closest to the kitchen had been knocked over and a few framed photos were littered near him. He stooped low to examine them and exhaled in a sharp sigh.

"What is it?" Mike asked, coming to join him.

"It's Kenny," Bill said quietly, pointing to the large frame in the center of the pile. It was a school portrait, complete with the photographer's name—*Hardscrabble Studios*—embossed in gold foil in the bottom right corner.

Kenny was smiling at the camera, his sharp features and dark hair offset by the pale blue backdrop behind him. Bill remembered that smile. He even remembered the horribly ugly sweater the boy in the photo was wearing, the one Roger always called Kenny's *Cosby sweater*. It was like looking through a window into the past.

"God, I hated that sweater," Mike muttered wistfully.

"So did Kenny," Bill added with a dry smile. "I think it was a gift from his mom. He always wore it when he wanted to look nice, but I swear he couldn't wait to get it off and back into the drawer."

"Oh man," came Hank's voice from behind them. "I haven't seen a picture of him in years." Bill and Mike turned to look up at him, and the expression on their faces was all he needed to see. "The house is clear. Steve's not here."

"Not here?" Bill asked in disbelief, standing back up. "Where do we look, then?"

"No clue," Hank replied. "It was a crapshoot just to get us here. I thought we'd have found him here, but unless you guys can think of something, I think the trail is cold."

Mike glanced at the photo of Kenny again. *I'm sorry*, he thought. *I'm sorry for everything.* He stood back up, and as he did so, he remembered his conversation with Kenny's father and Joe Ravenwood at the Midtown Café. Suddenly, the pieces began to fall into place.

"I know where we can go for help," he said, pointing the toe of his shoe at the stack of magazines Bill had been looking at earlier.

"Where?" Hank asked.

"Joe Ravenwood," he replied. "Daniel does work for him, and I saw them together on Sunday afternoon at the Midtown. They seem tight, and I have a feeling Mr. Ravenwood might know where to look."

"Works for me," Bill said. "A lead is a lead, right?"

"Exactly," Hank added, glancing at his watch. "Lets move fast, though. My guess is that Ravenwood's office will close at 5:00 p.m. and it's nearly ten-of right now. If Steve's still alive, he's probably on borrowed time. We need to get to him soon, or he'll be dead before the night is over."

CHAPTER THIRTEEN

Hank drove quickly and they made it to downtown Hollesley with two minutes to spare. After parking the car, they ran to the door of the Ravenwood Realty office, Hank leading the way.

They were met at the door by a woman in her late fifties who seemed to be leaving. She wore dark slacks and a floral blouse, and a pair of glasses hung from her neck on a gold chain. Bill, ever the connoisseur of stereotypes, thought she looked every inch a secretary.

"We're closed for the day, gentlemen," she said politely, holding up the keys as if they were some kind of talisman. "I would be happy to schedule an appointment for the morning, though."

Hank pulled his identification out as fast as a pistol and flashed it to her. "We're taking the last appointment of *this* day, ma'am. We need to talk to Mr. Ravenwood."

The woman opened her mouth to speak and then shut it again. Then she pulled the door wide and motioned for them to step inside. "Mr. Ravenwood is in his office packing up for the evening," she said with a slight quiver to her voice. "Let me tell him you're here."

The secretary vanished around one of the corners in the office entryway, and Hank looked at the others.

"I've never met this man," he said. "Mike, do you think you can take the lead on this?"

Mike nodded. "Absolutely."

He felt the guilt—his daily companion for two decades—writhing in his gut. He had a fleeting notion that if he could help save Steve, he could begin the process of exorcising this demon. Nothing could bring Kenny back, but taking action to save another friend might bring enough absolution to make a difference.

He turned his attention to the office around them. The flooring appeared to be marble, and the desk that greeted clients was crafted of a glossy slab of granite resting on small pillars joined with drywall. The name of the agency, Ravenwood Realty, was engraved on a large silver plaque along with the image of a bird. Mike assumed it was a raven.

Hank and Bill had taken a seat on one of the two pale blue sofas that flanked the foyer, though both of them looked far too nervous to sit still. Mike chose to stay near the desk, waiting for his chance to contribute.

When the woman returned, she seemed to have regained her composure. "Right this way, gentlemen,"

She said with a smile, and then beckoned them to follower her down the hallway.

Mike followed closely behind her as she led the way, and the others followed. The hallway was lined with framed certificates and awards, lauding the virtues of Ravenwood Realty. It reminded Mike of a Chevrolet dealership, where a blind man could toss a stone and have a very good chance of hitting a five-star award from GM.

The last door on the left was open, and the secretary stopped and ushered the men inside. Joe Ravenwood stood at his desk across the room and waved to the woman.

"Thank you, Susan," he said. "Lock up on your way out, if you wouldn't mind. I'll see you in the morning."

"Very good, Joe. Goodnight," she said, nodding to Mike and the others, and then she pulled the door closed behind her.

"Mike, right?" Joe said, extending a hand.

"That's right, Mr. Ravenwood. Thanks for seeing us. I realize it's unexpected, but we need to ask you some questions."

"*We?*" Joe replied, and then looked at the other men in the room.

Hank stepped forward and showed the man his ID. "Lieutenant Detective Phillips, Massachusetts State

Police," he said. "I'm here unofficially at the moment, but we need your help. This is our friend Bill McCarthy. Mr. Ravenwood, a man's life may depend on the information that you can share with us. And time is of the essence, as you might expect."

"I see. Very well." Ravenwood looked taken aback, but he did not press the issue. He waved his arm across the desk and offered the three other men a seat. Mike took him up on the offer, while Hank and Bill chose to pace at the back of the room.

"What can I do to help?" the man asked.

Mike leaned forward, elbows on his knees, and opened his hands disarmingly. "We're looking for Daniel Tobey."

"Daniel?" Ravenwood asked. "Why Daniel?"

"Because we think he might have been involved in a murder yesterday," Mike replied.

"Murder?" Ravenwood exclaimed, leaning forward. "Are you positive? Daniel is certainly—how should I say this?—an eccentric man. Some have considered him to be unstable. But I find it hard to believe him capable of killing someone."

"We're very certain," Hank said from behind Mike. "We're beyond the point of proving his guilt or innocence. What we need to know now is if you know anything about where he might be, or if you've noticed anything unusual or out of the ordinary about him lately."

Ravenwood sat for a moment in silence. He didn't look like a man trying to craft a lie or an argument, though. He simply appeared to be searching deep for something that fit the request.

Mike understood how guilt worked. If Daniel really was a killer, then there would have been clues. Odd behavior or unusual experiences that could have tipped off an observant friend. If Ravenwood didn't feel guilty for missing those signs yet, he sure would soon. And helping out was an easy way to ease that guilt.

"Out of the ordinary," he muttered. "You gentlemen don't know Daniel Tobey very well, then, do you?" he asked.

"Honestly," Bill responded, "no. We grew up with his son, Kenny. When Kenny died, we lost contact with Daniel. He's very much a stranger to us now."

"I see. Well, Daniel is a complicated man with eccentric interests."

"*Eccentric*. You've used that word already," Mike said. "What do you mean by that?"

"Daniel is a Native American, did you know that?"

"No, I didn't," Mike replied, glancing back to the others. "I don't think Kenny ever mentioned it to us, either."

Hank shook his head and Bill shrugged as if to say, "That's news to me."

"He's not only Native American," Ravenwood continued, "but also descended from a line of shamans dating back centuries within the Wampanoag people."

"Shaman?" Hank asked. "You mean, like a medicine man?"

Ravenwood chuckled and shook his head. "No, not at all. A shaman is more of a spiritual leader for a tribe. They speak to the Great Spirits, and are the keepers of the songs and stories of our people. In many ways, they serve as cultural guardians. It is a noble calling. Daniel became shaman when he was a young man, after his father died. He has always tried to live up to the expectations of his people. It is a difficult role."

"I get the feeling that Daniel is not the most ideal person for the role, then?" Mike asked.

Ravenwood sighed, as if releasing something held back until now. "No, I'm afraid he's been something of a black sheep to my people. Daniel has a very romantic yet broken view of his responsibilities. And when his son died, any hope we had for him to mature into his role vanished."

"A black sheep? How so?" Hank asked.

"He has an unhealthy interest in what my people would call *black shamanism*. He follows some of the teachings of a movement that began in the late nineteenth century called the Ghost Dance. The belief was that by performing certain rituals and dances, one might be able to summon a helper that would remove the white man from our lands."

"Sounds like witchcraft," Bill said.

"It is, and it's forbidden," Ravenwood replied. "But he's obsessed with it."

"What kind of behavior would his attitude lead to? What have you seen or heard that might cause you concern?" Mike spoke gently and tried to avoid anything that would push too much guilt toward the man.

"Please understand," Ravenwood said, "the elders of our tribe can only do so much. Daniel is an adult and a free man, and his personal time is his to devote as he chooses. We have, for the most part, turned a blind eye to his interest in black shamanism."

"For the most part," Hank said roughly. "So what *have* you seen, Mr. Ravenwood?"

Their host sighed again, and studied the surface of his desk for a moment before responding. Mike checked his watch and saw that it was nearly 5:30 p.m. Time was quickly slipping away.

"What I am going to tell you will sound like fantasy and superstitions, so please do not think me to be a foolish man. I am not sure I believe most of the legends of my people, but I'll let you be the judge as to how they might relate."

"Go on," Mike motioned with a hand.

"My people tell a story about a race of little people who live in the forest. They are called the pukwudgies, and their relationship with the Native Americans of New England is tenuous. They're similar to what northern Europeans might refer to as goblins or trolls. They cause harm to people, and never let go of a grudge when crossed."

"Puk-what?" Hank said, pulling a small notebook from his pocket to write the information down.

"Pukwudgies, Detective Phillips," Ravenwood said. "They are said to be small, maybe the height of a child, and very ugly. Some of my people believe that the Ghost Dance is a path toward contacting these creatures and drawing them into the service of a shaman."

"And these creatures are dangerous, then?" Hank asked, scribbling in his notebook.

"Very," Ravenwood replied. "I'm not suggesting that they are real—although the volume of stories about them among my people seem to suggest that there was at least a common root to the legend—but I am suggesting that if they *were*, they would be very risky to deal with."

Bill stepped toward the desk. "What do they look like?" he asked.

Ravenwood spread his hands apart. "It's all guesswork, honestly. Most stories speak of gray skin, long noses and ears, and red eyes. Some stories say it can become a porcupine, and others say it just resembles a troll. They wear rough clothing and don't speak, but they understand our languages very well."

Bill shivered. *Those red eyes*, he thought. *Red and sharp and looking right at me from the bushes.*

"Can they be killed?" Bill asked bluntly.

Ravenwood forced a smile. "You speak as if they were real, Mr. McCarthy."

"There's a chance, however remote, that one of our friends is currently a captive of Daniel's," Hank said, "and a few of the clues we have found suggest some kind of supernatural creature. We have found quills at the scene of three separate attacks. *Quills*, Mr. Ravenwood. Just like you, I have a hard time excepting this, but the evidence points to something that resonates with your stories."

"I don't know what to say," their host replied. "I've never been a superstitious man. This is outside of my realm of knowledge."

"Mr. Ravenwood, can they be killed or hurt?" Bill asked again, more urgently this time.

"Copper," he replied. "Some of the tales mention copper as a material that can harm them. But remember, these are legends dating back a thousand years or more.

Copper was hard to come by. I would assume it was added later as the story grew. I'm not sure I can give you that information with confidence in its accuracy."

Bill nodded. "Understood, thank you."

"Where can we find Daniel?" Hank asked. "Did any of his unusual behavior involve someplace special for him? Some place he might have felt safe to take a hostage?"

Ravenwood shook his head slowly. "I'm afraid I have no answer for you. Daniel has worked for me for years. He's a hard worker and has a fine attention to detail. I've worked with other carpenters over the course of my career, but Daniel's attention to detail and dedication to the job is exemplary. And that means I rarely see him outside of one of my properties, or this office."

"You had coffee with him yesterday, though," Mike added.

"Ah, yes," Ravenwood replied. "We frequently meet at the end of a project to discuss what I need from him next. Sometimes those meetings are held here, and sometimes we go and get coffee. It depends on my schedule and his availability. Yesterday we met at the café because he said he was already close to downtown and it was convenient to both of us."

"Was he finishing up a project near here?" Hank asked.

"No, I'm not sure what he was doing," Ravenwood replied. "Though, he certainly looked as if he had been working."

Mike paused for a moment. Something about what Ravenwood said had tripped an alarm in his mind and he turned his thoughts inward to find the reason. And then, like a light switch being flipped on to illuminate a dark room, he found the answer.

"Dust," he said out loud. He turned to look at Hank and Bill, and waited for them to catch his meaning. When neither did, he tried again.

"The dust, guys! Didn't you see it at the house?" Bill shook his head, but it seemed to register with Hank. "There was a jacket on the back of a chair at Daniel's house, remember? It was covered in dust. And so were the clothes he was wearing yesterday when I saw him at the Midtown."

"Dust from what?" Bill asked, confusion on his face.

"Not from what," Mike replied. "*Where*."

Recognition clicked with Hank and Bill at the same time, and they both blurted out the answer in unison. "Clements!"

"The old factory?" Ravenwood asked, not understanding.

"The abandoned Clements place, the place where Kenny died twenty years ago. The dust was too rough to be modern sheet rock. I think he's been working in there. Why, I have no idea. But that's where we need to look."

Hank was already heading toward the door, and Bill quickly followed along. An idea occurred to Mike, and he pulled one of his business cards out of his wallet. He then turned back to Mr. Ravenwood and extended the card to him.

"You've been very helpful, Joe. We really appreciate everything you've shared."

"Glad to help," he said uneasily, taking the business card from him. "Is there anything I can do for you? Anything to help?"

Mike shook his head quickly. "I'm not even sure what *we* can do to help, but it's our problem, not yours. If we're wrong, though, and you see Daniel—"

Ravenwood cut him off. "Don't worry, I'll call you immediately if I see him."

"Mike, come on!" Hank called out from the hallway.

"Thanks," he said again to Joe, and then ran out of the room to join them.

* * *

Mike climbed into the back of the car as fast as he could, but Hank pressed his foot down on the accelerator before he was able to shut the door. It swung back and slammed shut, just missing his foot.

"Easy, Hank," Mike called out.

"Are you sure about this?" Bill asked from the front seat.

"Positive," Mike said. "I think I'm the only one of us who has obsessed over every detail of the day Kenny died for the last twenty years. I'm certain of this."

"You put too much blame on yourself, man," Bill said. "We were all there. It wasn't just you in that place."

"Oh, I know that," Mike replied. "It was my idea, though. I'm the one who suggested we all go there. I had the lantern, and I'm the one who led us down into that lower room. If I hadn't been around that day, I don't think you guys would have gone there."

"Kenny wasn't a puppet, Mike," said Hank, joining in. "He made the choice to follow along. We all did. You're beating yourself up about something that you had no control over."

"Guys, it was my fault," he said, dismissing their attempts to vindicate him. "But I'm going to set it right. Steve can be saved. We're going to stop this."

"I hope you're right," Bill said. "But I'm not sure how. If this imaginary creature is real, and it's been killing our friends, then what chance do we stand?"

"What do you mean, 'if'?" Mike replied. "You don't believe the evidence?"

"A troll-like creature that lives in the woods and serves the whims of a black shaman?" Bill said incredulously. "Come on, Mike. Does that sound even remotely possible?"

"Bill, have you ever met someone who wears a coat made out of porcupine quills?"

Bill let out a nervous laugh, but Mike continued.

"Okay, so let's say someone in Salem—or the entire North Shore area, for that matter—actually has a coat made out of quills. That might possibly explain what we've found, but I'll say that the odds are very, very long, right? Now, what are the chances that this rare individual is also someone strong enough to rip the head off of a dog, willing to set a man on fire, and yet small enough to jump on your back and feel like a child?"

"Hey now," Bill said. "Don't mock me. I had a real experience."

"He's not mocking you," said Hank. "I think he's making sense. There is a big difference between forcing our own opinions onto the evidence and allowing the evidence to speak for itself."

"Exactly," said Mike. "Think this through, now: what you are suggesting is that there's a real, live person out there doing these things, even though the odds are totally against it."

"Well,—" began Bill, but Mike continued.

"When you remove the supernatural explanation as an option, that's the kind of theory we're left with. And I don't know about you, but I like the odds that we're dealing with some sort of a supernatural suspect much better. Whether it's this pukwudgie thing or not, I don't know, but the evidence points in that direction."

Mike looked out the window and saw that they had turned down Mill Street, the short road that led to the old Clements factory. There were few houses on this road, but he could see the lights through the windows as they passed by.

At the end of the road, their path was blocked by a large gate, part of the chain-link fence that surrounded the property. It had been installed shortly after Kenny's death, an attempt by the city to prevent further accidents before the mill could be demolished. But that day never came.

Hank stopped the car and got out to inspect the gate. He came back a moment later and opened the truck. When he reappeared, he had a large pair of bolt cutters. A moment later, the large gate was swinging open.

"Check this out," Hank said, tossing the lock to Bill as he climbed back into his seat. "Notice anything odd about it?"

Bill turned the lock over in his hand and noticed what Hank meant right away. The surface of this lock was clean and unweathered, and light played off it as if it had just come from the store.

"It's new," he said. "Newer than the fence, at least. Why would this be new?"

"My guess?" Hank replied. "I think Daniel needed an easier way to come and go at the mill than climbing the fence every time he wanted in."

"So he installed his own lock," Mike replied. "So, how long do you think he's been coming here?"

"No idea," Hank said. "But let's hope that he decided to come here tonight. If Daniel's not here, I'm not sure Steve has a chance, if he's alive at all, that is."

"He's here," Mike muttered, looking out the window into the darkness as they continued down the road. "There's no other place he would rather be."

"Why is that?" Bill asked. "This building is the site of the most painful event of his life. If it were me, I would avoid this place like the plague."

Mike forced a smile. "Some people can't let go of the past that easily, Bill. I think Daniel would rather live in the past for the rest of his life than face the future. That's what he and I have in common: neither of us can let go."

CHAPTER FOURTEEN

Night was fully upon them when Hank pulled the car onto the property that surrounded the old factory building. There was little pavement left, most of it having been reduced to crumbling debris by decades of New England weather. The lot wasn't completely abandoned, though; in one corner, closest to the building, was a large dark shape.

It was Daniel's old Ford Bronco. He had parked it near the large doorway that gapped out from the brick side of the structure. The doors long since pulled from their hinges and cast aside or rotted into oblivion. It seemed to wait for them like a wide, toothless mouth, ready to swallow them whole.

Hank killed the engine and the three men climbed out. The old lot was thick with silence, and if it hadn't been for the lights across the river that they could see through the trees, one might think that they were in the middle of nowhere.

Mike was having a difficult time coming to terms with where they were standing. Yes, it had been his idea to come here to look for Daniel and Steve. Having now actually returned to the sight of his greatest regret, he felt nothing but deep remorse and fear.

He was content to hang back and watch the building while Bill and Hank walked to the trunk of the car. Something about this place made him feel oppressed and tormented, as if it might strike out and try to hurt him.

Hank pulled a shotgun from the trunk and loaded it from a box of shells before stuffing the rest into his pocket. The gun had a tactical light attached to the end of the barrel, but he reached for a larger flashlight and handed that one to Bill.

"I can't arm you," Hank said apologetically. "It's bad enough that I'm doing this without my department's knowledge, but handing you a weapon would put the final nail in my career. You'll have to be happy with this thing, but it's heavy and would work well as a club in a pinch."

Bill nodded nervously. "I understand. If we're lucky, we won't need that." He pointed to the shotgun, but he had little hope in what he had said. Daniel was a cornered animal now, and cornered animals always fought back.

Hank closed the trunk and gave one last look at Bill. "You ready, man?"

Bill swallowed hard and nodded, and then they walked over to Mike, who was still lost in thought.

"Mike," Hank said questioningly. "You with us?"

Mike nodded numbly.

"We're going in. Stay behind me, alright?" With that, he headed off toward the doorway.

Mike didn't say anything, but simply turned and followed Bill into the darkness of the building. Passing through the doorway was like slipping into an ice bath; chills ran down his spine and gooseflesh broke out on his arms.

Ready or not, here I come, he thought.

* * *

The last time any of them had been inside the Clements building it had been a bright and sunny autumn afternoon. The large, high windows that lined one side of the building had acted like skylights then, allowing all of the light to flood in and fill the space. It had given the main interior a feeling of openness, like a massive cavern.

Now, though, under a shroud of darkness and two decades of bitter memories, the place seemed oppressive and confining. Without light to spill in through the windows it was difficult to see where to go. It was so completely black that Bill was sure he finally understood what it was like for someone who was blind. He made a mental note—ever the researching author—to bring that realism into one of his future books.

Hank was the only one of the three who moved with any semblance of confidence. Though it was probably thanks to the tactical light attached to the barrel of his shotgun, Bill suspected that the man's experience and training helped as well. He and Mike followed Hank through a maze of work tables and charred boxes that littered the floor, and every time the big red-haired man turned a corner and moved the light, a small amount of panic lurched up in Bill's chest.

A few minutes into their journey he remembered that Hank had given him a light of his own. He found it where he had left it, tucked into his belt against his lower back, and pulled it free. The small rubber dot on the shaft covered a switch, and when he thumbed it, light filled the aisle in front of him.

They moved slowly through the interior of the building, and that made it difficult to guess at the distance they had travelled. They might have walked halfway in, or barely scratched the surface; Bill couldn't tell, and that was playing with his senses. All he was aware of was the glow of light around their feet and the sounds of Mike following close behind. Everything else was numb and muffled.

Hank turned another corner, and Bill followed, glancing back to see if he could see Mike just in case his friend had stopped. He brought the flashlight level and saw that Mike was just a pace or two behind him. Bill nodded, and Mike nodded back. His face was set like stone.

A noise caught his attention. Whatever it was, it was neither in front nor behind them. It sounded as if something small and metallic had been dropped on the concrete floor a few yards away. Bill saw Hank's light stop and pan the area around them, and he brought his around to do the same. The skeletons of tables and shelving appeared in the glow of their lights and then vanished just as quickly. When they didn't hear it again, they continued on.

A moment later, something else moved in the darkness. This time it sounded like a piece of wood had toppled to the floor, maybe from one of the many work spaces they were weaving in and out of. Hank scanned the area again but, like the last time, he failed to notice anything out of the ordinary.

"Daniel!" he shouted into the darkness, which seemed to stifle the sound and reduce it to a whisper. "We know you're here, Daniel. We know what you've been doing."

A third sound, this time from somewhere to Bill's left, came as if in response to Hank's call. It was the sound of scuffing on the floor. It reminded Bill of the sound that a dog's paw makes when walking on tile. It was the sound of claws.

"Keep moving," Hank whispered harshly from the front of the line, and Bill felt Mike briefly bump into him and then apologize.

"Did you hear that last sound?" Bill asked him.

"Yeah," he replied. "Sounds like there's an animal in here with us."

Bill swallowed. He had been hoping it was just his imagination, but Mike's confirmation swiftly killed what little hope he had left. "Thanks," he said, without an ounce of gratitude.

They moved forward again, and Hank and Bill continued to occasionally sweep the area with their powerful lights, illuminating the debris and sea of countless tables. Hank still moved slow enough for the others to keep pace, but his steps had sped up slightly.

Then he tripped. Bill watched it happen from just a few feet behind. One moment his friend was walking slowly, shotgun raised in front of his chest, and then he was falling forward. Bill lurched and tried to catch him, but he was too slow. Hank landed hard and his gun skidded away, stopping a few feet ahead of his hands.

"You alright?" he asked as he knelt beside Hank, sprawled out on his stomach on the floor.

"Yeah," Hank hissed with frustration. "I must have tripped over something. I was sure my path was clear, but I must have caught my foot on something."

The big man climbed back to his feet, brushed off his knees, and then walked over to retrieve the gun and light. As he did, Bill heard another sound out in the darkness. This time it was to their right, and it seemed much closer than before. So close, in fact, that he saw Hank snatch the gun off the pavement quickly and bring it up, ready for action.

"What was that?" Mike hissed from behind them. "Guys, there's something out there, and it's getting closer."

Hank turned around to look at the others. "Closer? No, I think it's been nice and close this whole time. I think it's getting more *bold*."

"Bold?" Mike replied. "You mean, whatever it is out there is intelligent?"

Hank nodded in reply. "It's hunting us."

"Guys," Bill said, looking over Hank's shoulder. Then he pointed. "I see light."

All of them turned and immediately saw it; a dim rectangle of yellow light less than twenty yards ahead of them. It looked for all the world like a doorway, partially open to the space they were walking through.

Hank turned back. "Alright, that's got to be where Daniel is hiding, hopefully with Steve. Just stay behind me. And move carefully; I don't want any more accidents on the way."

Bill nodded and followed quickly after Mike and Hank. Fear was gripping his bowels like a vice. He wondered what he was more afraid of, the unknown creature in the darkness or the psychopathic man waiting for them in the next room. Neither sounded like a better choice, if he was honest.

Hank increased his pace, and they passed between dozens of work tables as they closed the distance between themselves and the light. They had walked no more than ten yards, though, when something struck Bill from the side, knocking him into a pile of blackened shelving.

"Bill!" cried Mike.

The weight of whatever had collided with him wasn't substantial, but it was solid and that caused him the most pain. The flashlight also slipped free from his hand and went crashing along the floor until it was far out of reach. As quickly as it had struck him, the animal—if that's what it really was—was gone. A moment later, the light from Bill's lost flashlight went out.

"Look out!" Hank shouted, and then the interior of the factory space erupted with the sound of shotgun fire. Bill thought he saw a shadow pass through the group, and then it was gone.

"Are you alright?" Mike said, leaning over to help pull some of the debris off of him.

Bill tried to stand, and a pain shot through his side. "Damn," he said. "I think I broke a rib."

"Here, grab ahold," Mike said, letting his friend put an arm around his shoulder before raising him to his feet. "Think you can walk?"

Bill nodded. "Yeah, it just hurts to breathe. No big deal, right?" He forced a playful smile.

Hank backed up toward them, still sweeping the darkness for whatever it was that had attacked them. Without turning around, he whispered over his shoulder.

"You guys okay?"

"We'll be fine," Mike said. "Bill think's he broken a rib, but he's not being too big of a baby about it yet."

Bill forced a smile, and then shifted his weight, trying to move some of the pain out of his head.

"Good," Hank replied. "Let's keep moving. I don't like not being able to see that thing coming, and I'll guarantee that it's going to come back soon."

The three men moved onward, Bill and Mike following after Hank and the small patch of pavement that his light exposed. The noises around them ebbed and flowed, sometimes rising to a clamor. The air smelled heavy with dust and mold, and there was something else as well. Something earthy and sickly sweet.

The bright light spilling from the room ahead of them was only a few yards away when another dark shape passed overhead. Bill flinched away, trying to duck under it, and the pain from the broken rib shot through his side like a spear. White light momentarily blurred his vision and he staggered, almost tumbling over.

Mike caught his elbow and helped him stay on his feet. He could see his friend's face by the light from the room ahead that was giving off a dim glow. They were both nervous, that was clear. Mike seemed overwhelmed, but that was understandable. He nodded a thanks to him and followed after Hank, who was already a few steps farther down the aisle between two long work tables.

"Guys," Mike said from behind him. Hank turned at the same time Bill did, and Mike pointed over his shoulder. "I think I just saw eyes out there."

"What color?" Bill asked. He knew the answer before Mike gave it.

"Red, I think," he replied. "What in the world has red eyes?"

Hank glanced into the dark, as if something was about to materialize right in front of them. After a moment of waiting, he motioned for the others to step in front of him.

"I'll take the rear from this point on," he said. "You guys should be able to see well enough until you get to the door. Just don't go in before me."

The others nodded and moved past him as he had suggested. The concrete floor of the old mill was much more clear now in front of them. Everything was covered in a thick layer of dust, and small bits of rubbish cluttered the area. The wreckage from the fire so many decades ago was still evident, but the years had muted it, like a snowfall muffles the sounds in a neighborhood.

The air cracked with another blast from Hank's shotgun. Bill wheeled around to see his friend taking aim at a small dark shape a few feet off the path.

"What is it?" he asked.

"No clue," Hank replied without turning around. "Damn thing is getting way too brave for my taste. Move faster. I'll keep up."

At their new pace, it was less than a minute later that they reached the doorway. Bill moved aside for Hank to take point. The big man leaned quietly against the doorframe and then glanced carefully into the room. Bill could see the light from the room splash across his face, seeming to set his red hair on fire. Then, with a wave of his hand, he led them in.

The room was small, no more than a dozen paces in either direction. Some of the walls were lined with metal shelving, and a large flat table was still standing at one end of the space. It could have been a storage room when the factory was operational, but history had erased most of the clues. The dust that covered everything in the building was here as well, and much of the exposed wood in the room was black and cracked.

New work had been completed, though, and Bill suspected it had been due to the efforts of Daniel Tobey. A small generator sat in the far corner, though the hum was surprisingly low and subtle. A work light hung from the ceiling a dozen feet above, powered by a yellow cable that ran to the generator. The table was covered with a mixture of odd tools, dozens of lit candles, an old gas lantern and what looked like a small pile of feathers.

Standing beside the table, lit by the yellow glow of the lamp above, was Daniel Tobey. His back was to them, but Bill could see that he wore only faded jeans and a gray flannel shirt. He stood over a large bundle on the concrete floor that was obscured by his shadow, and a long knife hung loosely in his hand.

Bill and Mike stepped into the room and took in the scene, staying slightly behind Hank, who immediately brought his gun up.

"Drop the knife, Daniel," he said with a calm, authoritative voice. "This ends now."

Daniel didn't turn around. For a moment, Bill wasn't sure if the man had even heard Hank speak. Then they heard the laughter, low and raspy, and it sent a chill down Bill's spine.

Daniel turned to face them. His face had been painted with red blocks, and a few feathers hung in his tangled hair. His eyes were wide and white, and his lips were pulled back to expose his teeth. Bill noticed how his forehead and neck glistened in the light and wondered if the man was nervous or distressed. Daniel's calm stance and even breathing told him otherwise, though.

"You think you caught me, Hank?" he said. His voice was measured and even. "You think you cracked my puzzle and came to frighten me away?"

"I came to take you into custody," Hank replied. The gun didn't move. "Again, drop the knife."

Daniel laughed again, his eyes never squinting, never leaving Hank and his shotgun. His hand twitched, but the knife remained in his grip, perhaps even tighter than before.

"You're here because I led you here," he said. "You're here because I wanted you here."

"We're here for Steve," Mike spat. "Where is he?"

Daniel glanced at the shape behind his feet. "Oh, he's here, don't worry. You're all here now. Just like I planned."

"You didn't plan this," Hank said, raising the shot gun to eye-level and taking aim. "You're not going to stand there and tell me you planned to be caught in the act. You'd have to be insane to think we're here because you wanted us here."

"Oh, but I am," Daniel replied. "I'm not insane, no. But I *am* certain you followed my trail. You three were the ones I couldn't kill in public. You three were the tricky ones, too visible to take out the easy way."

"Why's that?" Hank asked, the gun still pointed at Daniel.

"You're a police officer and you still need to ask me that question? *Tisk, tisk.* Bill and Mike are easy, right? Mike is nearly always at work, and that makes it hard to get him out into the darkness. Bill, well, I tried, but he figured out how to get away, it seems. And you," he said at last, bringing the knife up to point toward Hank, "you're a cop, constantly surrounded by other cops. Killing you *might* have been the hardest."

I figured out how to get away? Bill thought. *What does he mean? I was lucky, that's all. I couldn't even run straight, and I cried like a baby.*

"Might have been?" Hank replied.

"In public, sure," Daniel replied. "But here, on my ground, you're nothing but prey. And I am the hunter."

Bill stepped forward. "That's a lot of work just to kill us," he said. "Why now? Why here?"

Daniel chuckled, but it did not sound like the laughter of a sane man. "My son died twenty years ago in this very building. Twenty years of pain and grief and loss. Twenty years of waking up in an empty house. I lost my son!"

His shout was guttural and wild. Bill recoiled and took a step back. Beside him, Hank was less put off, but he blinked and the barrel of the gun twitched slightly. Daniel's laughter faded into a whimper, and his fingers tightened on the knife.

"My son," he whispered, "I lost my son."

"We all lost Kenny," Hank replied. "But that doesn't justify what you've done. Nothing could justify that. George and Roger were Kenny's friends, too. Steve was Kenny's friend. All of us were."

"Don't you dare use his name," Daniel hissed at them. He took a step forward, but Hank tightened his grip on the gun, giving him pause. "You all killed him. You. Not me. And you all deserve to die for it. Some of you already have," he said, and then motioned toward Steve's unconscious form, "and some of you will soon."

"I don't think so, Daniel," Hank said. "For the last time, drop the knife."

Daniel's lips peeled back in a grim, terrible smile. "I think it's time to end this. I brought you here to die in the dark, alone and afraid, just like my son. It's time to pay for your deeds, boys."

Hank stepped forward, ready to pull the trigger, but a sound behind him stopped him in his tracks. Bill and Mike heard it too. They turned just in time to see two shapes step in from the darkness of the main room.

"What the—" Mike began, but he was cut off. Both of the creatures opened their mouths and snarled viciously. The sound, like a dying wildcat, was terrifying, and all three men took a step backwards.

The creatures were short, no taller than a child, and incredibly gruesome. Ragged brown fabric shrouded most of their bodies, but their exposed skin was pale and wrinkled. Sharp teeth flashed from behind their thin, snarling lips.

Bill saw Hank spin back toward Daniel, who was now skirting the wall to move past the three men. Hank took aim and fired, but Daniel was faster and the shot missed, hitting the old stone wall behind him. Fragments of brick ricochetted backward into the room.

Hank fired one more shot as Daniel slipped out the door, but he couldn't tell if the shot was true. Beside the door, the two small creatures were crouched low, their brown cloaks pooled around them. Their eyes, bright red and glaring, seemed to be studying the men.

Bill and Mike staggered backward to move deeper into the room, away from the creatures, each of them kicking debris as they went. Bill's foot connected with an unseen object, and heard something metallic skitter across the floor and glanced down. *Was that a chisel?*

The creatures began to advance toward them. Hank glanced at the door once more, then at the others, and finally pulled a pistol from the shoulder holster under his jacket. After turning it over in his hand, he extended it toward Mike, grip-first.

"Take it," he said. "The safety is already off. I need to follow Daniel." He sounded desperate. "I can't let him get way."

Mike nodded, and then numbly took the handgun from Hank. It was heavier than he had thought, and it felt alive. He knew that was just his fear, but it didn't help settle the rising sensation of nausea in his gut. He had never held a gun before, let alone fired one, and his inexperience was almost paralyzing.

"Shoot them!" Hank shouted.

His words were like a slap in the face. Mike quickly leveled the gun at one of the creatures and pulled back hard on the trigger. The resulting sound was deafening in the small room, but the shot struck home. The creature closest to the door stumbled back, a dark hole appearing between its eyes. At the same instant, Hank was able to slip quickly out of the room, bolting after Daniel.

Bill took another step backward and tripped over another old tool, this one encrusted with dust and the blue-green corrosion that was the hallmark of old, weathered copper. He stared at it for a moment, and then, like a shot out of the darkness, a memory resurfaced. Something *had* been different about the night of the attack in his yard; he had used a tool on the creature. A *copper* tool. Ravenwood had mentioned copper, hadn't he?

The remaining pukwudgie took a step forward. Mike fired another shot at it but the bullet missed, exploding off the stone wall behind it. It didn't flinch, though. It simply hissed angrily at them, exposing its vicious teeth, and then moved closer. Less than a yard separated them now.

"Bill, I need ideas," Mike said with panic after pulling the trigger yet again. He struck the monster in the left arm, but it barely staggered before continuing forward. "It's almost here."

Bill bent to pick up the tool and felt more pain shoot through his side. He took in a sharp breath and then pushed through the discomfort to stand up straight again. When he looked at the object he had grabbed, its purpose almost didn't register. He had been expecting another chisel, or something else more common to his toolbox back home. The long, thin point of this new tool was something he had never used, though.

It was an awl. It resembled a short icepick, but he knew that it was used to punch holes in leather. A common item in the workshop of a shoe factory, perhaps, but it was completely new to Bill. The sharp point, though, quickly gave him the idea that he had been looking for.

"Get behind me, Mike," he said. He had one arm crossed over his chest against the pain, but the other brought the awl up slowly, like a knife. "I think I know what has to be done."

CHAPTER FIFTEEN

Hank stumbled out onto the dark factory floor, his shotgun moving from side to side in search of Daniel. For a moment he feared that the man had slipped away for good, and then a faint light caught his eye farther into the main space.

He moved swiftly after him, toppling shelfs and charred wooden crates as he rushed toward the end of the factory's interior. His quick steps kicked up clouds of dust, and the noise from his pursuit echoed around him. Within moments he had reached his destination.

The only doorway at this end of the building, as far as the light on his shotgun could reveal, lay directly in front of him. Hank froze at the sight of it, however, completely unable to move. It was massive and wide and full of darkness, and he recognized it instantly. This was the same room they had entered twenty years ago, the room that led to the stairs.

Dammit Hank, move!

He urged himself forward, but shivers were creeping up his neck. Time had certainly helped him leave this place behind, but he had somehow returned. Though every fiber of his being cried out against it, he knew he now had to relive those painful memories. If he was to stop Daniel, he would have to follow this path into the dark heart of the building.

As soon as he entered the space, he noticed that the room was dramatically different from the last time he had been inside. The emergency response team that had worked so hard to find Kenny that day, fighting against all odds to try and save him, had used the space as a staging zone for their rescue efforts. What they left behind had changed the room in many ways.

The two tables he remembered had both been broken into pieces and pushed to the far corner, and piles of stone and dust flanked the far doorway. In place of the tables against the wall to his right, though, was something that was eerily familiar: a metal door.

Of course Hank recognized it. This was the large metal door that had once hung from broken mounts at the bottom of the stairs. The door that had fallen on Kenny, instantly killing him.

Perhaps the rescue personnel had wanted to remove it from the building, like taking the door off of a broken refrigerator before dropping it off at the city dump. Maybe it had simply gotten in their way during whatever construction had taken place to reinforce the structure of the room below. Regardless, there it was, leaning against the wall like a dark monolith.

The floor around it was covered in tools and plastic bags from the local hardware store. One bag even hung from one of the large bolts that protruded from its rusty surface. Hank was certain, though: it was clearly the same door.

A flicker of light caught his eye. *Daniel must have a light with him down there*, he thought. *Doesn't he know that the room below is a dead end?*

He held the shotgun cautiously in front of his body and slowly walked toward the stairway, giving the metal door a wide berth out of fear and superstition. However irrational it seemed to him, he expected it to come crashing down on him, crushing him as it had Kenny so many years before. Nothing happened, though, and the only change he noted was that his heart was beating much faster than before.

A faint light reached out from below, casting long shadows on the stairway walls. There could be no mistaking it now; Daniel was down there, waiting for him. Knowing it was most likely the worst idea he had come up with yet today, he swallowed hard, adjusted his grip on the gun, and began the descent.

The stairs felt different beneath his feet. Hank remembered them being covered in debris from the deteriorating concrete, and how the lead edge was weathered and broken. These, though, felt new and sturdy. He pointed the light at his feet and immediately understood why. They had been repaired.

He was unsure what to do with this new piece of information. Clearly, Daniel was the one who fixed the stairs. No one else had reason to come here and do random work on a derelict factory. What gave Hank reason to pause, though, was *why* Daniel would have done this.

Two reasons seemed most likely: he either wanted to travel safely down to the site of his son's death on a regular basis, or he had some other, unknown purpose for the room. A purpose that possibly involved Hank and his friends.

Both options disturbed him. If Daniel had done this work because he wanted to visit his son's figurative tomb, then he was much more mentally unstable than Hank had expected. He was a single dad who worked far too many hours to be social. In his infrequent time with him, though, Daniel never struck him as an unstable person.

If, on the other hand, this was all part of some long-term, premeditated plan to trap Kenny's old friends in the basement of the mill, then everything Daniel had said made even more sense. He really had intended for things to happen just as they had today. Did that make him crazy, though, or just very driven?

Hank couldn't help but feel manipulated. Being a puppet for other people was something he had always hated. Given the opportunity, he always preferred to call his own shots and make his own decisions.

Whatever the reason for the repaired steps, he was certain that he had good reason to keep his guard up. Resigning himself to the difficult task ahead, he descended the stairs slowly, gun trained on the faint glow spilling through the open doorway at the bottom.

* * *

Bill tumbled backward and Mike cried out in fear and surprise. The creature had jumped quickly toward them and caught Bill squarely on the chest, knocking him down. Rather than rolling off, though, the pukwudgie clung to Bill and began to claw at him.

Mike staggered back and brought his gun up, aiming it right at the monster's back.

"Are you crazy?" Bill shouted. "You'll shoot me!"

He had one of his hands on the creature's chest. There was so much power in its small frame, and it took everything Bill had to keep it from clawing at his face and throat.

Mike tried kicking at it, but lost his balance and fell back against the wall. The gun fell from his hand and skidded across the cement floor into one of the corners.

"What can I do, Bill?"

"Copper," Bill panted, struggling under the grasping arms of the creature. "Find something made of copper!"

He swung with the awl and slashed a deep cut across one of the creature's arms. It howled and flinched backward, the light in its red eyes flashing bright and fierce. Bill struck again and this time slashed across its chest. A third blow cut at one of the clawed hands trying to slash at his throat.

The pukwudgie was learning, though, and it began to avoid Bill's swipes with the awl with unnatural agility. His next blow missed high, and the creature slipped beneath the sharp tip of the weapon. In the moment that it took Bill to bring his weapon around for another strike, the creature moved in and slashed out with one of its gray hands. The awl, Bill's only hope of salvation, skittered away and rolled out of reach.

The small, troll-like monster flashed a wide grin, as if pleased with itself, and then lashed out with a fury. This time the sharp claws of its small, boney hand raked across

Bill's chest, tearing his shirt and flesh beneath it. Cold pain flashed before giving way to a warm sensation. It was his own blood, spilling out of the wound and down his side.

He cried out with pain and tried to roll onto his side, hoping it would topple the creature and give him a chance to get away. Instead, the pukwudgie rolled with him, and then turned and clamped its mouth around Bill's left forearm. Sharp, needle-like teeth penetrated the skin and muscle of his arm, and he could feel the bones inside slowly grinding under the pressure.

Mike had fallen back against the wall and had pulled his knees up to his chest. His eyes were locked on the creature, but they were vacant and unfocused.

"Mike!" Bill shrieked at his friend.

Mike stirred, and for a moment he looked as if he were waking up. Then he screamed. Deep and loud and guttural, the scream filled the small room and the walls vibrated with the echo. He turned toward the wall, pushing with his legs in a vain attempt to move farther away from the scene he was witnessing.

Bill cried out in pain and swung the fist on his free arm at the head of the creature that was locked tight on the other. The blow connected, and it felt like he had struck a mellon. The pukwudgie's mouth opened for a moment and Bill quickly pulled his arm free before striking out with both fists, catching the creature directly in the center of the chest.

It flew backward onto the dusty floor and Bill scrambled backwards to put distance between them. Something stopped him, though, and he turned to see Steve's unconscious body laying directly behind him. His friends hands and feet had been tied, and there was a small pool of blood near his chest. Steve needed help, but judging by his limp form and bindings, he wasn't going anywhere soon.

A small yet incredibly strong hand grabbed his foot, and Bill looked to see the creature staggering to its feet. A couple of yards away, Mike was doing the same, leaning against the wall and attempting to push himself to his feet. Bill kicked out, trying to dislodge the clawed fingers on his heel as panic washed over him. And then the pukwudgie launched itself forward, directly at him.

It landed on him in a flurry of sharp claws and gnashing teeth. Bill let out a horrified shriek and pushed himself backward against Steve's body while the monstrous thing on his chest continued to thrash like a drowning cat, complete with high-pitched growls. He brought his arms up to protect his face while trying to slap away some of the blows that the creature was landing on him.

And then it stopped.

One moment Bill had been doing everything he could to dodge the claws that were shredding his stomach and arms, and the next it had abruptly ended. The creature sat upright and stared vacantly over his head, arms falling to its side like wet ropes. Then, slowly, it leaned to the side and tumbled over.

Behind the pukwudgie, standing over Bill's legs, was Mike. He held the copper awl in his left hand and a thin ribbon of blood was dripping off its sharp tip.

"Thanks," Bill whispered. It was all he could manage. Pain was everywhere, and his chest and midsection were on fire.

"I—," Mike began. "Sorry that took me so long." He reached out with his free hand and offered to help him up.

Bill took the hand and winced as his broken rib and dozens of bloody gashes in his chest cried out against the movement. He stood in silence beside his friend for a moment, and began to think about what they needed to do next.

"Hank probably needs us," he finally said, though the tone in his voice made it clear that he wanted nothing more than to get out of the building and run.

Mike waved a hand at Steve, laying quietly on the floor. "What about him?"

"He's not going anywhere," Bill replied. "Those things are dead. The only real threat now is Daniel, and Hank is off somewhere alone with him. We should go help him."

Mike sighed again, and then nodded. "But I'm bringing this." He held up the bloody awl for Bill to see.

"You won't get an argument from me," he replied, and then walked over to the table to grab the lantern.

It was green and covered in dents and scratches, but Bill couldn't help but notice that it was nearly identical to his father's lantern. He quickly used one of the candles to light the wick.

They were about to turn and walk out of the room when a loud, sharp noise echoed through the building. Both men turned to look at each other, the blood draining from their faces.

"Was that a gun shot?" Mike asked.

Bill didn't answer. Instead, he dashed for the door. Mike followed right behind him.

* * *

Hank moved off of the last step and and through the doorway into the lower room. Instantly, pain shot through his head and he felt himself toppling sideways toward the floor. He landed hard, striking his head against the pavement, and heard his shotgun clatter away from his reach.

He opened his eyes and saw the ceiling above him. It was a spider's web of wooden beams. Some were dark and cracked, but some were pale and relatively new. They all seemed to overlap and lead back to the doorway, where a large strut had been placed above the threshold, held up by a large metal post on either side of the stairs.

It took him a moment to realize it, but what he was seeing was not the work of Daniel, but the emergency response team that had struggled to safely get inside the room and retrieve Kenny's body. They had done their best to shore up the collapsing doorway and ceiling in an effort to clear out the debris and reach the boy trapped inside.

"Oh, you prick," Hank moaned, rolling to his side as fast as his throbbing head would allow. "You're going to fight dirty, is that it?"

Daniel stepped out of a shadow on the opposite side of the doorway and moved swiftly toward him. He brought one of his feet, clad in a brown leather work boot, back behind him and then shot it forward, aiming for Hank's ribs.

Hank was faster, though. He caught the foot inches before it connected with his side, and pushed the man backwards. Daniel stumbled for a moment and then found his balance again.

"Oh, I don't need to do anything, Hank. In just a moment, my little helpers are going to return and finish you off for me." He grinned at the detective who was standing up, one palm pressed against the side of his head. "They should be finishing up with your friends upstairs right about now."

Hank dragged the side of his hand across his mouth, wiping away spittle tinted red with blood. "You've got this all planned out, don't you?"

Daniel smiled, and it sent chills down Hank's spine. The man was clearly insane. Whether he had been driven there by the death of his son, or by the dark magic he had been toying with, Hank had no idea. But he was certain that either way, the man needed to be stopped.

"You talk about planning," Daniel replied, "but I prefer to think that it was destined to end this way."

A scream broke through from above them, echoing through the walls of the building. It was loud and horrifying and Hank recognized the voice immediately. It was Mike.

"Ah." Daniel smiled, more than a little pleased with himself. "Right on schedule. It won't be long now before you are screaming just like that."

Another less powerful scream rang out a moment later, and Hank turned to look up the stairs. Though it was quieter, he could still tell that this scream belonged to

Bill. The harsh, painful realization that he might very well be the last of them alive swept over him and he closed his eyes and swayed on his feet.

In that instant, the older man made his move. He dove toward the floor, near where Hank had fallen. Before the detective could stop him, Daniel was standing back up, the brilliant light of the shotgun shining directly in Hank's eyes.

"I thought you were waiting for your helpers," Hank said. The tone of his voice mocked the other man. "If they don't get here soon, you might have to do the deed yourself."

"Oh, they'll be here," he replied, but Hank could hear the uncertainness in his voice. If Mike and Bill had succeeded in beating those things, it was only a matter of time before they came to his aid.

Hank needed to think quickly to find a way out of this situation. He was unarmed, injured and standing with his own weapon pointed at his head. While his friends might be coming to help him at this very moment, they might also be dead on the floor beside Steve, the creatures who killed them moving swiftly toward the lower room.

He found his answer in the past.

"You know," he said, stepping back one more step, "I'm not a writer like Bill, but I find it almost poetic how you're going to die on the very same patch of concrete that your son did twenty years ago."

The light from the shotgun moved as Daniel lowered it to lock eyes with him. "Don't you *dare* speak about my son," he growled. "My son is dead because of you. *You.*" He emphasized the last word by pointing the gun back at Hank like an accusatory finger.

"Daniel, you've had a long time to tell yourself that. But Kenny was a big boy. He agreed to come into this place. Was it a dumb idea? Absolutely. Do I regret going along with it? Of course I do. But Kenny died because he decided to walk into this room. No one dragged him in here and forced him to stand still while the door fell on him. Kenny did it all himself."

Daniel's face slacked, and the emotional pain was clearly visible. There was something else, though. Hank could sense it. Was it possible that Daniel didn't know?

"Don't tell me," he said. "You didn't know how Kenny died? What did they tell you? That he was crushed to death in this room?"

"Stop it!" shouted the man with the gun.

"Daniel, your son was crushed beneath a massive metal door. The door upstairs that you've been using to hang your shopping bags on."

His words hung in the air like dust, oppressive and suffocating, and Daniel began swaying on his feet. The shotgun was no longer a weapon, just an object that now hung limply in his hand. Hank didn't have to strike out at him with a weapon; his words had done everything a blade would have done. Possibly more.

"Your son," Hank continued, driving home the emotional knife, "died right there." He pointed at a patch of old, dusty concrete just two feet to the left of Daniel.

The man's face was twisted with grief, and tears had streaked through the red war paint on his cheekbones. He turned to look at the spot that Hank had pointed out, and that's when the detective moved.

"Liar!" Daniel shouted when he saw the detective lurching toward the door. He brought the shotgun back up and pulled the trigger. "Liar!"

The wall to Hank's right exploded as the shot missed him. He felt a cloud of small, sharp fragments of stone spray the side of his neck and face. He no longer had time to think, and simply trusted that his plan would work. Taking one last breath, he dove to his left.

His shoulder connected with one of the metal posts that had been installed by the rescue team, the ones designed to hold up the new lintel over the doorway. He felt the bones of his arm and shoulder collide with the post, and the pain nearly blinded him.

Hank pushed harder, though, and he heard the foot of the post scrape against the concrete floor. Another shot exploded from the gun and a small portion of the wall in front of him shattered violently.

He cast one last glance at Daniel, who stood a few feet away with the shotgun upraised. The man was an emotional tempest, with tears drawing shimmering lines across his twisted, painted face. Then, with amazing speed, Hank lifted one foot and kicked out hard at the base of the post. He felt his ankle break at the same moment the post slipped free, and he dove painfully into the stairway behind him.

The sound was tremendous. The lintel over the threshold fell free, and the stone and mortar that had been held in place by it came spilling out in an eerie repeat of the past. Everything went dark as Hank limped up the steps as fast as his left foot would allow him. A cloud of dust billowed up from beneath him as if it were in pursuit.

He mounted the steps painfully, unsure when he might reach the end, and nearly collided with the wall at the top. At the last moment, light spilled into the stairway, enough to make him slow down and turn into the room. In doing so, he nearly ran Mike and Bill over.

"Hank!" Bill shouted. "What's happening?"

The floor beneath their feet moved and trembled. Earthquakes are rare in New England, though they do happen. This, though, wasn't an earthquake, and all three men knew it.

"Daniel's dead," he said through clenched teeth. "We have to get out of here. I have a feeling the whole building is going to come down this time. And I think my ankle is broken."

A piece of the ceiling a few feet to their right dropped to the floor as if to confirm Hank's prediction. Dust was raining down from every seam and joint above them, and the tremors continued to grow.

"I'll help Hank," Bill said decisively, moving closer to slip an arm under the big detective's shoulder. "Mike, you're going to have to get Steve before this place comes down on top of him."

Mike nodded but inwardly he fought back intense panic. They were going to trust *him* to save Steve? Mike, who had let Kenny die so long ago? Mike, who couldn't save George or Roger? It was now up to him, and that frightened him more than anything.

"Mike?" Hank barked. "You with us?"

He nodded.

"Good," Hank replied. "Listen, follow us until we get to the room Steve is in, and then we'll head out with the lantern and get the car's headlights pointed into the building. That should create enough light for you and Steve to find your way outside."

Mike nodded again, and Bill helped Hank limp toward the door and out into the main factory space.

Mike followed behind as they made their way carefully between old burned tables and shelves, until they reached the room where they had first found Daniel.

"Move fast, guys," Mike said as they limped onward. "I'm going to need that light as fast as you can get it turned on."

"We're on it," shouted Hank over his shoulder.

Mike watched them for a moment longer, and then ran into the room as another tremor shook the floor beneath him. A piece of the wall and ceiling in one of the corners crumbled and spilled to the floor, and dust began to fill the air.

The generator was still humming along off to the side, and the yellow glow of the work light felt safe. That wouldn't last long, though, and Mike knew that. The generator could get buried under a pile of rubble at any moment, and he had to get Steve out before that happened.

Steve, surprisingly, was waking up. His eyes were glassy, but he seemed to be aware of his surroundings. Mike ran up and dropped down beside him.

"This place doesn't look so good, Mikey," Steve said, glancing over his friend's shoulder. "You're going to get me out of here, right?"

Mike nodded and studied his friend. Daniel, or one of the creatures, had cut his midsection enough that he had bled all over the floor. Remembering the blood on the driveway at Daniel's house, he assumed the injury had happened there. Steve seemed alert, but he was too pale. He had clearly lost too much blood.

"I'll get you out of here," he said. "You know how good I am at saving people, right?"

"Kenny wasn't your fault, man," Steve said weakly. "And I don't want to heap too much pressure on you, but this might be your chance to redeem yourself, whether or not we think that's necessary. Because trust me, I don't want to die today."

Mike ran to the table and dug through the tools. "Ah!" he shouted, and came back with a small utility knife. "This should do it."

The rope cut away quickly, and Mike helped his friend up as more pieces of the ceiling fell down around them. They paused for a moment, clasping hands like two business partners shaking on a deal, and then bolted for the door.

Steve was slower, but he did his best to keep up. His injuries were significant, but they weren't preventing him from running. Of course, the quickly disintegrating building served as a wonderful incentive to get out as fast as possible.

The view through the door into the main area was pitch black, and Mike's mind filled with doubt that his friends were going to be able to give him enough light to escape by. Just as they were passing through the doorway, though, a bright glow filled the room on the far end of the building.

It wasn't perfect, but both men could see the tables and shelves well enough to navigate their way out. Mike pointed toward the source of the light, and the large doorway in the far wall of the building, and shouted for Steve to follow him.

It only took moments. With the building crashing down around them, Mike and Steve ran as fast as they were able, crossing the factory floor in a blur. Stone and wood fell with a growing intensity, and the sound was deafening.

Small pieces of debris rained down all around them, striking them on the head and back. Larger chunks fell onto the ancient work tables, breaking them into pieces, but miraculously none landed on the two men. Steve only tripped once as he tried to maneuver around a toppled tangle of shelving, but Mike quickly pulled him back to his feet and toward the exit.

Finally, as an enormous portion of the main ceiling gave way, they passed through the large doorway and into the warm night air.

EPILOGUE

A thin layer of snow had recently covered the Whale's Jaw. It looked like one of those cheap cotton tree skirts that people had used to cover the base of their Christmas trees just two months ago. It was untouched, being so high up off the ground. Bill wondered, were he to climb atop the boulder now, if he would find bird tracks in wandering rows, or would it be pristine and virgin.

Dogtown wasn't the safest of places anymore, with the odds much higher of encountering a drug addict rather than a bird watcher. In a place once known as the Common Settlement, what was common now was graffiti, drugs, and alcohol. Some might add witchcraft to that, but the truth of that statement would hinge heavily on your definition of what exactly is *considered* witchcraft.

Winter had a cleansing effect here. The cold and wind kept the low-lifes and addicts away, and the deep snow prevented most visitors from wandering too far off the path. Bill had noticed only one other set of snow shoe tracks on his way to the Whale's Jaw—one other, that is, besides his own—but the snow covered whatever signs there were of the darker activities.

He thought of liquid paper and correction tape for typewriters, and how a healthy layer of either could hide the mistakes and missteps beneath. It seemed just as true here, where the snow had erased, if even for a just one season, all that this place had become.

Bill couldn't help but wish it were that simple in all areas of life, but some mistakes and missteps were destined to leave their mark forever. Life was messy, and there was no magic corrective fluid to change that law.

Under his thick coat, under the sweater and long-sleeve t-shirt he wore, one would find all the evidence necessary to prove the existence of the messiness of life. Scars, long and jagged, crossed his chest like pink ribbons. Scars that had twins in his mind.

Bill glanced around at the untouched snow once more, and then removed his gloves and took a small notebook out of his back pocket. He unclipped the pen and jotted down a few notes. He took a deep breath and felt the air chill his throat and lungs, then watched as his exhale clouded in the air in front of his face.

It occurred to him how much the snow was like time, covering up so many of the details of the past. Wait long enough and most painful events become simply unpleasant, and then eventually there is nothing left of them but a bump in the snow.

Most events.

Some things were harder to forget. Kenny's death would never fade away entirely. George and Roger were still open wounds in his soul, plot threads left unresolved and cut by an unforgiving editor. And then there were the events of that night four months ago. They would never truly leave him, he was certain of that.

He and the others had met a few times since the autumn, grief therapy under the pretense of drinks with friends. They were never entirely unproductive gatherings, though. It was clear that each of them were moving forward and healing in his own way.

Steve, who spent most of his time inside the ruined factory unconscious and bound like a rodeo calf, had moved past their tragedy the most completely. He claimed to still have occasional dreams about those lights—pretty lights—in the land behind his home. When he would wake, it was often to a pillow damp with tears. When Bill asked him why, Steve was unable to tell if it was fear or sadness.

The doctor had finally removed the cast from Hank's ankle a month ago, and he was working with a physical therapist to regain the strength that his job required. He seemed different to Bill, though, somehow darker, more brooding.

He was perhaps the most independent of the group, and the most concerned with the rules and laws that governed the world. What transpired that weekend in October left a lot of those notions in crumpled heaps on the floor of his mind. He appeared to be getting by, but Bill sensed that there was quite a lot of confusion beneath the surface, like a man attempting to regain his bearings.

Mike, though, was the most transformed by what had happened to them. Bill had known his friend to be a man who anchored his identity in what he had failed to do. Kenny's death became his oppressor, one that abused him and mocked him and filled him with sick dread. Having to face that fear straight on in October had helped him process that guilt.

Bill wasn't sure he would ever say that Mike was a healed man. But he did know this: whatever he had to endure that night, whatever haunts and demons he forced himself to face, they had made him stronger. Mike was— Bill dug deep for a word to package up his assessment— more complete, more whole.

They all seemed to be able to push forward and move on. At least, that's the impression he took away from their infrequent gatherings at the pub. Even Bill himself had made progress. His writer's block had crumbled shortly after the derelict factory had, and he completed the book in record time. *The Lovely Mrs. Walker*, his fourth novel, was now safely in the hands of Jean, his editor.

It was evidently good, too. Jean had told him repeatedly over the last six weeks or so that it was the finest piece of writing he had ever handed over to her, and quite possibly the best novel she had ever read. It smelled an awful lot like hyperbole to Bill, but he had since decided that he would allow the market to make the final declaration.

No, there was no magic liquid paper that could erase what he and his friends had experienced. But there was hope. Hope that it was all behind them. Hope that they could each become better versions of themselves as a result. And a hope that their friendship had been strengthened and fortified.

He put away his notebook and pen and then tugged his gloves back on. After one last glance at the enormous boulder that George and Kenny had once climbed so many years ago, he lifted one of his snowshoe-clad feet and turned back the way he had come.

If Bill had been asked that evening, he would not be able to say for sure, but he was convinced that for a moment he saw movement in the trees behind him. There had been nothing there when he turned his head to look, just the empty branches of the small trees that winter had stripped bare.

Those branches were no more than twigs really, fingers on the frail arm of a cluster of saplings. Even in the crisp, clean air of winter, though, Bill was struck by how much they resembled quills. Long, pale quills.

CPSIA information can be obtained
at www.ICGtesting.com
Printed in the USA
LVHW03s1421100718
583280LV00011B/592/P